Nur Baba

This first-ever English translation of *Nur Baba*—a classic of modern Turkish literature written by Yakup Kadri Karaosmanoğlu—offers a unique window into Sufi lodges, social dilemmas, and intellectual life in early twentieth-century Istanbul.

Inspired by Karaosmanoğlu's personal experiences with Islamic mystical orders, it is a story of illicit romance and spiritual inquiry, depicting a colorful lodge of Sufi dervishes led by a charismatic, yet morally suspect, spiritual master named Nur Baba. The plot follows his attempts to seduce an attractive married woman from an elite family and recounts her dramatic experiences in the life of a Sufi community. The setting shuttles between the grand mansions of Istanbul's elite families and a Sufi lodge where rich and poor intermingle. Exploring questions of gender, morality, and religious bias throughout, it captures the *zeitgeist* of early twentieth-century modernist thinkers who criticized Sufism for impeding social progress and debated the public roles of women in a rapidly modernizing society.

Alongside the editor's meticulous translation, the volume includes a scholarly introduction, maps, and images, as well as explanatory footnotes that will aid both students and scholars alike. The novel will be of particular interest to those studying world literature, Sufi studies, and Ottoman-Turkish history.

Yakup Kadri Karaosmanoğlu (1889–1974) figures among the most prominent Turkish novelists and writers of the twentieth century. Born in Cairo to a prestigious family, Karaosmanoğlu lived through the turbulent transition from empire to nation-state in the early twentieth century and emerged as a prominent author with an uncanny ability to capture the *zeitgeist* through fiction. His early novels probe the social crises and tensions of the late Ottoman Empire and the early years of the Turkish republic. In addition to being a prominent public intellectual, he served several terms as a member of parliament and worked for the Ministry of Foreign Affairs at a number of diplomatic postings.

M. Brett Wilson is Associate Professor of History and Public Policy at Central European University and the Director of the Center of Eastern Mediterranean Studies. He is the author of *Translating the Qur'an in an Age of Nationalism: Print Culture and Modern Islam in Turkey* (2014).

Routledge Sufi Series
General Editor: Ian Richard Netton
Professor of Islamic Studies, *University of Exeter*

The Routledge Sufi Series provides short introductions to a variety of facets of the subject, which are accessible both to the general reader and the student and scholar in the field. Each book will be either a synthesis of existing knowledge or a distinct contribution to, and extension of, knowledge of the particular topic. The two major underlying principles of the Series are sound scholarship and readability.

Published by Routledge

For more information about this series, please visit: www.routledge.com/Routledge-Sufi-Series/book-series/SE0491

Nur Baba

A Sufi Novel of Late Ottoman Istanbul

Yakup Kadri Karaosmanoğlu

**Edited, Introduced, and Translated by
M. Brett Wilson**

LONDON AND NEW YORK

First published in English 2023
by Routledge
4 Park Square, Milton Park, Abingdon, Oxon OX14 4RN

and by Routledge
605 Third Avenue, New York, NY 10158

Routledge is an imprint of the Taylor & Francis Group, an informa business

Originally published in the Turkish language under the title: *Nur Baba*
by Yakup Kadri Karaosmanoğlu

Copyright © 1983, İletişim Yayınları

This translation published by arrangement with AnatoliaLit Agency

Translated by M. Brett Wilson

British Library Cataloguing-in-Publication Data
A catalogue record for this book is available from the British Library

Library of Congress Cataloging-in-Publication Data
Names: Karaosmanoğlu, Yakup Kadri, 1889–1974, author. |
Wilson, M. Brett, translator.
Title: Nur Baba : a Sufi novel of late Ottoman Istanbul /
Yakup Kadri Karaosmanoğlu ; edited, introduced and translated by M. Brett Wilson.
Other titles: Nur Baba. English Description: Abingdon, Oxon ; New York, NY :
Routledge, 2023. | Series: Routledge Sufi series |
Includes bibliographical references and index. |
Identifiers: LCCN 2022057686 (print) | LCCN 2022057687 (ebook) |
ISBN 9781032463902 (hardback) | ISBN 9781032463926 (paperback) |
ISBN 9781003381471 (ebook)
Subjects: LCSH: Sufism–Fiction. | LCGFT: Novels.
Classification: LCC PL248.K3 N8713 2023 (print) |
LCC PL248.K3 (ebook) | DDC 894/.3533–dc23/eng/20230316
LC record available at https://lccn.loc.gov/2022057686
LC ebook record available at https://lccn.loc.gov/2022057687

ISBN: 978-1-032-46390-2 (hbk)
ISBN: 978-1-032-46392-6 (pbk)
ISBN: 978-1-003-38147-1 (ebk)

DOI 10.4324/9781003381471

Typeset in Times New Roman
by Newgen Publishing UK

In memory of my friend Vangelis Kechriotis (1969–2015), with whom I began my studies in this field.

Contents

Illustrations

Figures

Maps

Acknowledgments

It is with no small degree of pleasure that I witness the publication of this volume, which has taken me many years to translate, annotate, and arrange the formalities of publication. As is the case in such long-term projects, many people have contributed over the years, helping in smaller and greater ways to make this book possible. Their help has been particularly vital to this project as the task of rendering Karaosmanoğlu's late Ottoman-Turkish novel into English forced me, on many occasions, to seek the assistance and expertise of others.

This project began under the guidance of Erdağ Göknar at Duke University. Several of the initial chapter drafts, which were rough and no doubt excruciatingly painful to read, were composed in discussion with him. Erdağ's fortitude and patience in going through them was much appreciated, and, fortunately, the text has come a long way since that time. He is in no way responsible for the quality of this final translation but is infinitely culpable for encouraging me to continue with the project, despite the undeniable coarseness of its early iterations.

My doctoral advisee Merve Demirkan-Aydoğan took on the herculean task of going through the entire manuscript, line-by-line and word-by-word, in the last stage of the translating process. Her meticulousness and knowledge of Turkish proved to be immensely important, as her suggestions identified a number of problems and yielded sundry improvements to the quality of the text. She also contributed to the explanatory footnotes. Cem Kara generously read the Introduction and provided helpful comments on part of the manuscript. His knowledge of Bektashi studies proved invaluable for improving the information on the Bektashi order and its history. Cristina Corduneanu-Huci, my superior half, read through the final manuscript and provided helpful commentary and corrections that made the text more readable for non-specialists. At an intermediate stage in the project, Samara Reigh's edits improved the literary quality of the translation. Yusuf Selman İnanç was an excellent research assistant and found many valuable sources. Shahzad Bashir, Anne Blackburn, Giancarlo Casale, Sinem Arcak Casale, Nathalie Clayer, Ayşe Çelikkol, Markus Dressler, Carl Ernst, Tolga Esmer, Jan Hennings, Marlon James, Wesley Joyner, Mahnaz Kousha, Tijana Krstic, James Laine,

Bruce Lawrence, Ebrahim Moosa, Christoph Neumann, Kenneth Perkins, Matt Rahaim, Kevin Reinhart, Jenna Rice, Matthias Riedl, Charles Shaw, and my students provided much needed encouragement along the way for this seemingly never-ending project. I would like to thank my first teacher of Turkish language, Ceyda Arslan-Kechriotis, as well as my instructors in Ottoman Turkish: Yorgos Dedes, Selim Kuru, and Wheeler Thackston.

Firat Oruç, İrvin Cemil Schick, and especially Yektan and Zeynep Türkyılmaz deserve thanks for fielding my linguistic questions at different points in time. İrvin Cemil Schick generously provided images of Bektashi artwork from his personal collection and allowed them to be used in the book. Furkan Sevim of the Istanbul Araştırmaları Enstitütü provided timely assistance with several historical photographs. My former colleagues at Macalester College in the Department of Religious Studies and current colleagues in the Department of History at Central European University provided supportive and collegial environments in which to work and both institutions supplied research funding, especially ACRO at CEU, that was critical for the completion of this project. Joe Whiting at Routledge and Can Belge at İletişim very kindly dealt with all the legal arrangements that made this publication possible. Euan Rice-Coates handed numerous publication issues, and Jeanne Brady completed the copy-editing. I am indebted to Eda Güçlü and Murat Tülek who produced the maps. In the home stretch, Osman Kocabal assisted with finding images, assembling the bibliography, and compiling an index.

Note on Spelling and Pronunciation

With few exceptions, I have used standard modern Turkish spelling for place and personal names in Ottoman-Turkish and Turkish. Deference has been given to the spellings in the *Redhouse Türkçe/Osmanlıca-İngilizce Sözlük* (SEV, 1997). Technical terms have also been provided in this manner. The names of well-known figures with Arabic names (e.g., Muhammad) are spelled according to common English practice without diacritics. The reader unfamiliar with certain characters and their sounds in Ottoman and Turkish may use the following guide to approximate pronunciation.

â is an elongated "a" sound as in "ah" (e.g., Nigâr)

c is pronounced like *j* in "jump" (e.g., Celile)

ç is pronounced like *ch* in "chap" (e.g., Çinari)

ş is pronounced like *sh* in "shot" (e.g., Şişli)

ı is not present in English but pronounced similar to the *u* in "but" (e.g., Kanlıca)

ö is not present in English but is similar to the German *ö* in schön (e.g., Kadıköy)

ğ is usually silent in modern speech but elongates the preceding vowel (e.g., Beyoğlu)

ü is not present in English but pronounced like the German *ü* in über (e.g., Üsküdar)

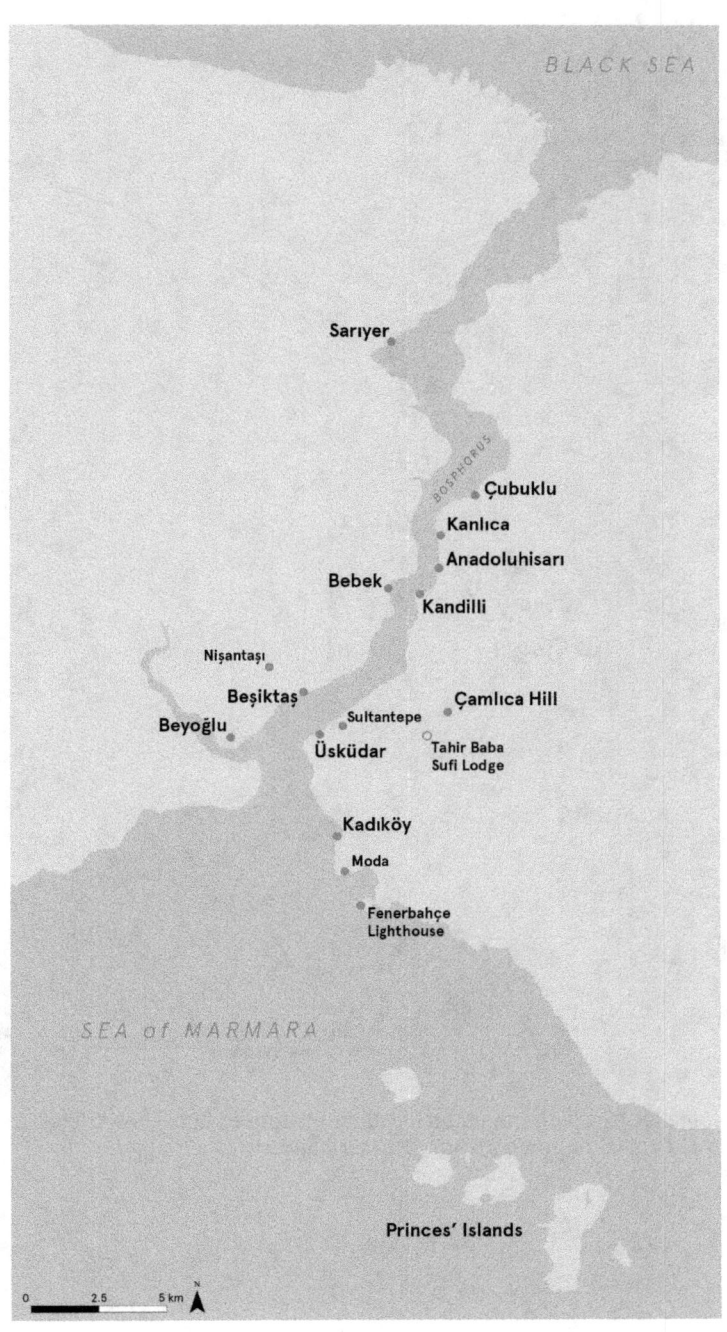

Map 1 Greater Istanbul with locations from the novel.

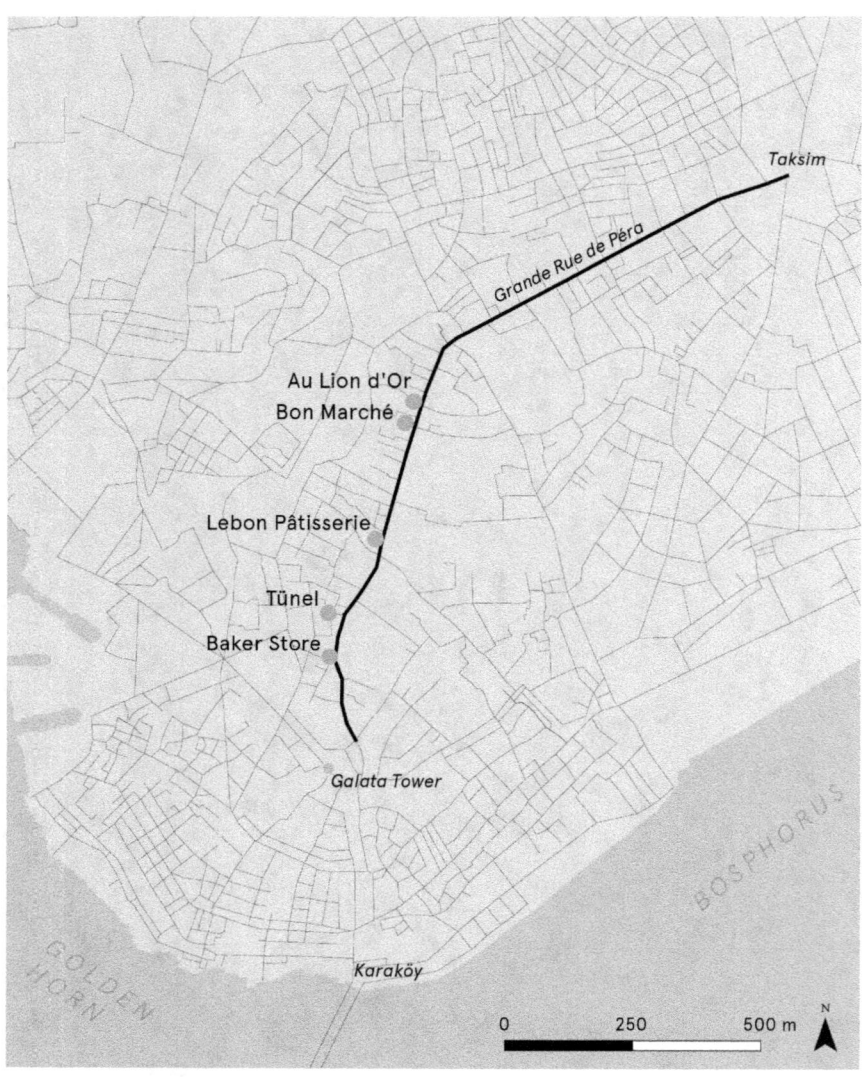

Map 2 Beyoğlu District with shops and locations mentioned in the novel. The Grande Rue de Péra is the contemporary İstiklal Caddesi.

Introduction

It may be said that Istanbul is drunk on the wine of *Nur Baba*.[1]

(Ahmet Hâşim)

One evening, Mustafa Kemal Atatürk (1881–1938) invited two leaders or *babas* of the Bektashi Sufi order to join him for an evening at the presidential mansion in Ankara. The President of the Turkish Republic enjoyed hosting and discussing various matters with intellectuals, politicians, and writers until late in the evenings. On this occasion, he wished to discuss the novel *Nur Baba* with representatives of the Sufi order described therein or, at the very least, to see if they resembled the colorful fictional characters. Rumors had been circulating at the time that one of the guests—Ali Nutki Baba (1869–1936), the last leader of the Tahir Baba Lodge in Çamlıca—was the basis for the charismatic yet sinister main character Nur Baba.[2] Along with the two Bektashi babas, a group of musicians was present, one of whom recorded the events of the evening. The musician writes:[3] We started to play music. After a few songs Atatürk asked Ali Nutki: "What are the distinctive characteristics of the Bektashi order?"

1 Ahmet Hâşim, "Yakup Kadri *Nur Baba* Münasebetiyle," *Akşam*, nr. 1305, 9 Mayıs 1338/May 9, 1922: 3.
2 Ali Nutki Baba had a number of links with not only the Istanbul literary elite but also with foreign residents of Istanbul who wished to join the Bektashi order. Kara describes several non-Muslims requesting initiation with him, upon which he did not look favorably without first converting to Islam: Cem Kara, *Grenzen überschreitende Derwische: Kulturbeziehungen des Bektaschi-Ordens 1826–1925*. Vol. 15 (Vandenhoeck & Ruprecht, 2018), 172, 219. This lodge is also known as the Tahir Baba Lodge, Nur Baba Lodge, and Çamlıca Lodge.
3 The following anecdote is adapted from: Sadi Yaver Ataman, *Atatürk ve Türk Musıkisi* (Ankara: Kültür Bakanlığı, 1991), 52–55. Bedri Noyan, has compared different stories about this evening in *Bütün yönleriyle Bektâşîlik ve Alevîlik: Vol. VI Ünlü Bektaşiler ve Bektaşi fıkraları* (Ankara: Ardıç Yayınları, 2003), 32–39.

DOI: 10.4324/9781003381471-1

Ali Nutki Baba replied:

"It is a social life that was established hundreds of years ago. Because of the fanaticism of those times when women and men were not allowed to eat and drink together, Haji Bektash set up a society like ours today, under the name of a mystical order."

Disappointed by this answer that was clearly designed to please the questioner, he turned to Haydar Naki Baba and repeated the question. He replied:

"The brother members of the Bektashi come to the dervish lodge on special days of the week and sit around the Baba in the evening. The ladies, led by the oldest lady member, sit opposite to the Baba and eat and drink from the table in front of them. This meeting continues with music, poems, and merry making."

Still not satisfied, the President turned to a more specific line of questioning: "There is something about a cupbearer. What is that?"

"It is the most important subject of the Bektashi feasts. Bektashis drink *rakı*[4] with closed glasses which means that the amount of *rakı* cannot be seen. Everybody has to drink *rakı* from the same glass. There is a connection between the Baba and the cupbearer who carries the glass from hand to hand. With a signal given by the Baba, an empty glass or a glass with less *rakı* is given to those who seem a bit drunk. According to the order's rules, the disciple cannot refuse this glass. The gathering continues with the same cheer and good spirit till morning."

Upon the President's request, music followed, but as the musicians began to play another tune, the President interrupted and asked:

"They say that [...] the book *Nur Baba* was written as a description of your private life. Is this true?"

Ali Nutki replied:

"Sir, this is a joke by Yakup Kadri. I lived a rather uneventful life among friends and disciples. And, well, after the closure of the Sufi lodges, I'm leading an absolutely calm life."

Atatürk turned to a member of his entourage and ordered him to invite the author Yakup Kadri Karaosmanoğlu to join them. Less than an hour later, he turned up at the presidential mansion and entered the room; "Upon seeing Ali Nutki, he was stunned." The alleged subject of the author's satirical, sensationalistic, even defamatory novel was sitting at the table. The novel had prompted the highest office of state to convene a rather uncomfortable meeting between a novelist and the Bektashi baba that had initiated him into the rites of the Bektashi path. Following this evening, Atatürk appointed Ali Nutki Baba to the position of *kaymakam* in the administration of the Anatolian locality of Mucur, not far from the tomb complex of

---

4 *Rakı* is an anise flavored spirit with an alcohol level between 38–50 percent, akin to *arak*, *ouzo*, and *pastis*.

Haji Bektash, where he passed away in 1936.[5] The novel that fascinated the President of the Turkish Republic remains a controversial and influential book to this very day.

The Lodge

On the steep hill of Çamlıca on Istanbul's Asian shore lies the graveyard of a Sufi lodge—the Tahir Baba Lodge—a place known in the early twentieth century for its association with a Sufi master and his colorful following of dervishes made famous by the novel *Nur Baba*.[6] In the late nineteenth century, under the leadership of Nuri Baba (1817–1892), the lodge began to be known as a place that brought together artists and writers as well as cultural and political elites, including foreigners and non-Muslims. The novel is set in this period, the 1880s or early 1890s, during the reign of Sultan Abdülhamid II, an era that Karaosmanoğlu and his generation associated with absolutism, censorship, and surveillance of civil society via a large network of informers.

Once a complex that included an orchard and several buildings, including a spacious mansion overlooking the Bosphorus, the only thing that remains now, in any recognizable form, is the graveyard in which some leaders and members of the order are buried, where, in line with the time-tested rule, stone outlasted wood. Like many Sufi properties, the Çamlıca Lodge complex fell into disrepair following 1925 and all its buildings were destroyed in the 1950s.[7] Most of the property has now been conquered by concrete apartment blocks. Of the lodge itself, little remains except the tombs and the novel that you now hold in your hands.

The Novel and its Various Controversies

Nur Baba is one of the best-known Turkish novels of the early twentieth century, written by one of Turkey's premier novelists, Yakup Kadri Karaosmanoğlu (1889–1974). Born in Cairo to a prominent yet diminished Ottoman family, Karaosmanoğlu lived through the transition from empire to nation-state and became a prominent journalist and author. His early novels, *Nur Baba* included, explore the social crises and tensions that occurred during the final years of the Ottoman Empire. Karaosmanoğlu distinguished himself

---

5 Fahri Maden, "Çamlıca'da bir Erenler Durağı: Tahir Baba Tekkesi," in *Uluslararası Üsküdar Sempozyumu VII: 1352'den Bugüne Şehir*, ed. Süleyman Faruk Göncüoğlu (İstanbul: 2012), 236–237.

6 Sometimes this lodge is referred to as the Kısıklı Lodge, Büyük Çamlıca Lodge, or Nur Baba Lodge.

7 Maden, "Çamlıca'da," 237.

as an innovator in Turkish literary modernism and played an important role in shaping the modern Turkish novel.[8]

Since its first appearance in the final years of the Ottoman Empire, the novel has been a source of controversy and debate. Its depiction of a sometimes festive, sometimes debauched Sufi lodge led by a manipulative, amorously inclined Sufi master was nothing short of a scandal for late Ottoman society. The elites of Istanbul gossiped and debated who the real-life individuals were that were the bases for the characters in the novel, particularly those female characters who fell in love with Nur Baba. A resident of Istanbul and the author of an important work about the Bektashi order, the American missionary-scholar John Kingsley Birge (1888–1952), scribbled in his personal copy of *Nur Baba*, "Hussein Bey tells me he knew the family described in this story."[9] Birge's book, *The Bektashi Order of Dervishes*, describes the novel as a "highly critical study in novel form of the Bektashi Way."[10]

The story was first published in serialized form in the newspaper *Akşam* in 1921, but the Foreign Ministry ordered its interruption due to its controversial content.[11] The controversy over the novel at the time was multifaceted. On the one hand, devotees of the Bektashi Sufi order objected to the defamatory and inaccurate portrayal of their community. The author and statesman Bezmi Nusret (1890–1961), for example, accused Karaosmanoğlu of intentionally inciting the public by intertwining religion with a sensationalistic and lascivious story that has nothing to do with the Bektashi Sufi order.[12] The novel was published as a book in 1922 and became an instant sensation, all copies of the first edition selling out within a few months. Soon after publication, it served as the basis for the motion picture *Secrets of the Bosphorus* (*Boğaziçi Esrarı*, 1922), directed by Muhsin Ertuğrul. During the shooting of the film version, a group of dervishes stormed the set, driving some cast members to abandon the film. Fearing unrest, the Allied occupying forces in Istanbul prohibited the film from being shown in theaters.[13] Another contentious characteristic of the novel was its depiction of and attitude toward women. The important novelist and writer Halide Edip Adıvar (1884–1964)

---

8 Ayşe Özge Koçak Hemmat, *The Turkish Novel and the Quest for Rationality* (Leiden: Brill Rodopi, 2019), 89–90; Erdağ Göknar, "The Novel in Turkish: Narrative Tradition to Nobel Prize," *The Cambridge History of Turkey* 4 (2008), 472–503.

9 Handwritten note of John Kingsley Birge, August 26, 1932. Personal Collection of the Translator.

10 Despite its age, Birge's study remains an indispensable introduction to the Bektashi order: John Kingsley Birge, *The Bektashi Order of Dervishes* (London: Luzac, 1937), 79.

11 *Akşam* published the story in installments from May 13 to July 22, 1921. Cafer Gariper and Yasemin Küçükcoşkun, "II. Meşrutiyet Döneminde Yayımlanan Nur Baba Romanı ve Yarattığı Akisler," *Bilig/Türk Dünyası Sosyal Bilimler Dergisi* 47 (2008): 47.

12 Bezmi Nusret [Kaygusuz], *Nur Baba Masalı* in Ahmet Demir, "Yakup Kadri Karaosmanoğlu'nun *Nur Baba*'sı için Döneminde bir Reddiye: *Nur Baba Masalı*," *Türk Kültürü ve Hacı Bektaş Veli Araştırma Dergisi* 80 (2016): 62.

13 Öztürk, Serdar. "Türk sinemasında ilk sansür tartışmaları ve yeni belgeler," *Galatasaray Üniversitesi İletişim Dergisi* 5 (2006): 62–63.

criticized Karaosmanoğlu's work as a degrading portrayal of women. The well-known author and literary critic Ahmet Hamdi Tanpınar wrote that in the novel we witness "the corruption of woman."[14] Contemporary readers will have little difficulty identifying passages that take an essentializing and critical view of female characters and women in general.

An important dimension of the controversy was the extent to which the novel was intended to be a depiction of reality. While Karaosmanoğlu insisted that it was a work of art, he also commented on the sorry state of Sufi lodges, implying that his fictional tale was an accurate reflection of real moral corruption in the lodges. The inclusion of the actual names of real historical figures in the novel, such as the author Muallim Nâci (1849–1893) and the Bektashi leaders Afif Baba and Nuri Baba, reveal the intertwining of fact with fiction throughout. He went further in his memoirs, explaining that he did not need to describe his experiences in the lodge because he had already done so at length in *Nur Baba*. Additionally, he recounts specific personal memories and events—for example, the celebration of the Nevruz (Nowruz) holiday[15] that he attended together with the poet Yahya Kemal (1884–1958)—which appear, almost unchanged, in the novel itself. Likewise, his description of how he began to attend the lodge in real life also corresponds precisely with the plot.[16] In the early 1970s, Yakup Kadri explained that the novel was a product of his personal disappointment with Bektashism after having attended a number of Bektashi lodges and taken initiation with Ali Nutki Baba at the Tahir Baba Lodge. However, he also comments that Ali Nutki did not resemble the fictional Nur Baba in most respects but was only the "raw material" out of which he created the character.[17] The novel is a work of literature inspired by the author's experiences, however embellished or transformed they may be, injected with historical details and content from an earlier period (1880–1893) during which Yakup Kadri had no connection with the lodge.

Many modernist intellectuals and statesmen in the late Ottoman Empire came to believe that, like other Ottoman institutions, the Sufi lodges were corrupt establishments that no longer fulfilled the cause of public good, but in fact impeded efforts to modernize society and caused no small amount of individual, familial, and societal damage. This idea comes through very clearly in *Nur Baba*. In Muslim communities around the world, similar ideas had circulated in reformist circles during the late nineteenth and early twentieth

14 Ahmet Hamdi Tanpınar, *Edebiyat Dersleri* (İstanbul: Yapı Kredi Yayınları, 2002), 45.
15 Nevruz: the Persian New Year festival, which is celebrated at the spring equinox, around the 21st of March. The Persian word "nevruz" literally means "new day." Bektashis believe that it also marks the birthday of Ali.
16 Yakup Kadri Karaosmanoğlu, *Gençlik ve Edebiyat Hatıraları* (Ankara: Bilgi Yayınları: 1969), 167–169.
17 Mustafa Baydar, "Karaosmanoğlu, «Nur Baba», Rıza Nur ve «Atatürk» üzerine açıklamalar yapıyor," *Milliyet* (December 20, 1974): 30.

century, placing modern scrutiny upon Sufi practices such as tomb visitation, master-disciple relations, and recitation ceremonies (*zikr*) involving music and dance-like motions such as whirling or spinning.[18] In the late Ottoman Empire, modernist critiques of Sufism focused on issues such as financial corruption, lethargy and laziness, bad hygiene the unpreparedness and lack of knowledge of Sufi leaders—especially those that inherited the position from their fathers—and sexual misconduct.

In 1925, three years after the publication of *Nur Baba*, a momentous event occurred when the Turkish Parliament banned Sufi orders, ceremonies, titles, and costumes and, moreover, confiscated all their properties and financial endowments. The immediate catalyst for the suppression of Sufi orders and lodges was the Shaykh Said Rebellion in 1925, an uprising in southeastern Turkey led by a Naqshbandi Sufi leader. The novel captures the intellectual and political zeitgeist surrounding Sufism and Sufi lodges prior to state intervention. Radical critiques of religious institutions had been brewing since the second decade of the 1900s when Karaosmanoğlu began composing the book. Ideas that were initially on the radical fringe—such as proposing the abolition of Sufism—found various forms of artistic and, later, political expression with the reforms of the first two years of the Turkish Republic during which the Parliament abolished the caliphate, closed the Islamic schools and courts, and shuttered the Sufi lodges and tombs.

In addition to being an engaging story about a Sufi quest gone wrong, *Nur Baba* is an excellent cross-section of the ideas about Sufism and Sufi lodges present in the final decades of the Ottoman Empire, particularly nationalist thought. Simultaneous with its critical gaze towards Sufi ceremonies and social habits, the novel is replete with enthusiasm for the idea that Sufi lodges are repositories of Turkish national culture that had been lost during centuries of Islamization and the adoption of Persian and Arabic forms of high culture. It must be kept in mind that the novel was composed during a formative period of Turkish nationalism, when intellectuals were attempting to excavate and define the nation with the cultural remnants they had at their disposal and no small amount of historical mythmaking. Sufism had great value for these imaginative miners of national culture. And of all the Sufi orders that were to be consulted in the quest for Turkish literature and folklore, the Bektashi Sufi order held a somewhat privileged position. In contrast to orders that used Arabic or Persian as ritual languages, the Bektashi order conducted most of its ceremonies in the Turkish language and had a large corpus of Turkish hymns and poetry. For this reason, nationalist intellectuals focused great effort

---

18 See, for example, Elizabeth Sirriyeh, *Sufis and Anti-Sufis: The Defense, Rethinking and Rejection of Sufism in the Modern World* (Routledge Sufi Studies Series, 1998); Carl Ernst, *The Shambhala Guide to Sufism* (Boston, MA: Shambhala, 1997), Chap. 8; Frederick de Jong and Bernd Radke, eds., *Islamic Mysticism Contested* (Leiden: Brill, 1999).

on researching Bektashis and, as can be seen in the novel, projected their nationalist imaginaries onto the order.[19]

The Bektashi Order

To aid the reader, a brief introduction to this Sufi lineage is fitting. The Bektashi order takes its name from the figure Haji Bektash (d. ca. 1271), whose tomb complex is in the central Anatolian district of Nevşehir, 180km southeast of Ankara. After its crystallization as a formal order in the sixteenth century, the Bektashi order was linked closely with the Janissary military units which were instrumental in the spread of Ottoman power.[20] Following a period of military losses and political involvement by the Janissaries, Sultan Mahmud II (r. 1808–1839) suppressed the Janissaries together with the Bektashi order in 1826, forcing Bektashism to operate clandestinely for several decades. While the Janissaries disappeared from the stage of history, the Bektashi order reemerged in the second half of the nineteenth century when the political climate permitted, and patronage from elites provided financial and political support during the reigns of Sultans Abdülmecid (r. 1839–61) and Abdülaziz (r. 1861–76).[21] Despite its *de facto* reemergence, the Bektashi order remained technically illegal until the end of the empire and most Bektashi lodges were officially Naqshbandi, operating in a state of ambiguity and rivalry with Naqshbandis over control of these institutions. Under Sultan Abdülhamid II (r. 1876–1909), a few lodges in the capital patronized by the upper classes became refuges for escapism and, allegedly, debauchery. The novel refers to these periods in late Ottoman history—the open festive times of Abdülaziz—and the dark repressive days of Abdülhamid II, indicating clearly that the story of *Nur Baba* takes place during the reign of Abdülhamid II, when some lodges were flooded with elite Istanbulites.[22]

The Bektashi order was subject to a number of stereotypes and prejudices, stemming from the fact that Bektashis practiced Islam in a way that did not always please the official Islamic scholars, the *ulama*. Bektashis are permitted to drink alcohol, have their own esoteric interpretation of the five pillars

---

19 Dressler's study deals at length with the fascination of nationalists with the Bektashi and the Kızılbaş-Alevi: Markus Dressler, *Writing Religion* (Oxford: Oxford University Press, 2013).

20 Founded sometime in the late fourteenth century CE, the Janissaries were an infantry unit and standing army whose legal status was that of slaves of the sultan (*kapı kulu*). They also played an important role as the imperial bodyguard. On the Bektashi order, see Birge, *The Bektashi Order* and *Bektachiyya: Études sur l'ordre mystique des bektachis et les groupes relevant de Hadji Bektach*, eds. Aleksandar Popović and Gilles Veinstein (Istanbul: Ed. Isis, 1995).

21 Nathalie Clayer, "Sufi Printed Matter and Knowledge about the Bektashi Order in the Late Ottoman Period," in *Sufism, Literary Production, and Printing in the Nineteenth Century*, eds. Rachida Chic et al. (Würzburg: Ergon-Verlag, 2015), 355.

22 M. Brett Wilson, "The Twilight of Ottoman Sufism: Antiquity, Immorality, and Nation in Yakup Kadri Karaosmanoğlu's *Nur Baba*," International Journal of Middle East Studies 49 (2017): 242–243.

of Islam, and hold ceremonies at which both men and women are present. Drawing on this last characteristic, the most famous slander accuses Bektashi ceremonies of conducting ritualized orgies. The libel proceeds as follows: men and women allegedly gather together in a ceremonial space and then the candles are put out, after which, in the dark, everyone engages in sexual acts with whomever they encounter. This orgiastic libel is known in Turkish as "putting out the candle" (*mum söndürmek*). The seventeenth-century Ottoman traveler Evliya Çelebi (1611–ca. 1684) describes the association between this sexual-religious slander and allegiance to the Persian Safavid Shahs:

> It is also reported about the province of Sivas [...] that they extinguish the candle and that everyone embraces another man's wife and lies with her in a corner—God forbid! This humble slave has traversed those regions often since the conquest of Baghdad (in 1648); and [...] I carried out several offices in Keskin and in Bozok; and I never observed anything like that.
>
> Again, these officious people claim that there are Shah-lovers and candle-extinguishers and men and women who wear the Shah's diadem in Rumelia, in the province of Silistria, in the districts of Deli Orman and Kara Su, and in the Dobrudja. As God is my witness, I have sojourned in those countries perhaps fifty times, and have carried out offices there, and I never observed any such illegitimate activities—although, to be sure, there are those who fail to pray, or who run after singing girls.[23]

Persisting until the present, the "putting out the candle" libel is ancient, stretching back at least as far as the Roman Empire's persecution of the Bacchanalia cult to the god of wine in the second century BCE. The myth of "putting out the candle" has been marshaled in the northern and eastern Mediterranean against many religious groups with clandestine rituals such as the early Christians, the Kızılbaş-Alevis, the Ismailis (in Syria), Sabbateans (the Dönmes), and Bektashis.

Karaosmanoğlu plays upon elements of this libel in the novel but never repeats it per se. For example, the first chapter is provocatively titled: "How Is the Candle Put Out in a Bektashi Lodge?" No Turkish reader could miss the connotation of this title, and, throughout the novel, he creates a social, ritual portrait with strong resonances of the Roman Bacchanalia, alluding to orgiastic fantasies and creating characters—such as the heroine Nigâr—with direct inspiration from the Bacchanalia. The ancient slander is evoked and combined with modern biases against Bektashis in such a way that creates the impression of a continuity of sensual, secretive religious rites—fictional or real—between ancient Greco-Roman mystery cults and the Sufi

23 Evliya Çelebi, *An Ottoman Traveller: Selections from the Book of Travels of Evliya Çelebi*, trans. and ed. Robert Dankoff and Sooyong Kim (London: Eland, 2011), 136–137.

lodges of early twentieth-century Istanbul.[24] In this way, the deep reservoir of Mediterranean religious slander achieves its late Ottoman, Istanbulite expression in the pages of *Nur Baba*.

Afterlife in Translation

The well-known scholar of Sufism Annemarie Schimmel (1922–2003) completed the first full translation of *Nur Baba* in a foreign language—German—published in 1947.[25] Given her notoriety as a scholar and the relative accessibility of German for European and American academia, her translation has served for some as a conduit to this important "dervish novel" for scholars and students.[26] In addition to German, the novel has been rendered into Greek, Slovak, Italian, Spanish, and Serbo-Croatian.[27] Despite a wide interest in this novel by European publishers and scholars of Sufism, the present work is the first English-language translation of this early twentieth-century classic. The boom in research on the late Ottoman period and increasing interest in Turkish literature and the history of Islamic thought make now a fitting time for an English language rendering. Rather few late Ottoman texts exist in English language translation, and, for the purposes of Sufi studies, there is a notable paucity of primary sources available from the late Ottoman and early Republican eras. I hope that this volume will be a useful source for students, scholars, and readers interested in Sufism, religion, nationalism, Orientalism, and mysticism in the late Ottoman Empire.

When translating any work of Turkish literature from the early twentieth century, the question of which source text to use is a matter of importance because many novels, including *Nur Baba*, were published first in the Ottoman script and then, after the transition to the modified Latin alphabet in 1928, in many subsequent versions. Editions of *Nur Baba* published after the alphabet change and the language reforms of the 1930s have minor discrepancies from the original text. In the main, these relate to the substitution of archaic words and phrases with more widely understood modern terms. This is a standard procedure in the post-1928 publication of Turkish literature that is called

---

24 Wilson, "Twilight of Ottoman Sufism,": 246.
25 Yakup Kadri Karaosmanoğlu, *Flamme Und Falter Ein Derwisch-Roman*, trans. Annemarie Schimmel (Gummersbach: Florestan, 1947).
26 References to the Schimmel translation are numerous: for example, Ernst, *The Shambhala Guide to Sufism*, 218; Gotthard Jäschke, "Die Frauenfrage in der Türkei," *Saeculum* 10. JG (1959): 360–369; Sarah Coakley, ed., *Religion and the Body*. Cambridge Studies in Religious Traditions, Vol. 8. (Cambridge, UK: Cambridge University Press, 2000), 262, fn.1; Annemarie Schimmel, *Mystical Dimensions of Islam* (Chapel Hill: University of North Carolina Press, 1975), 341.
27 Serbo-Croatian: *Nur Baba,* trans. Fetah Sulejmanpašić (Sarajevo: n.p., 1957); Slovak: *Derviš a dáma*, trans. Xénie Celnarová (Bratislava: Tatran, 1989); Italian: *Nur Baba*, trans. Giampiero Bellingeri Fabula (Milano: Adelphi, 1995); Spanish: *Nur Babá*, trans. Alín Salom (Barcelona: Destino, 2000); and Greek: *Ο τεκές του Νουρ Μπαμπά ή Κατήχηση στον έρωτα: μυθιστόρημα*, trans. Giorgos Salakidis (Thessalonikē: Stamoulēs Ant., 2009).

"simplification" (*sadeleştirme*), since, otherwise, contemporary readers would have great difficulty understanding early twentieth-century language. In some instances, the occasional phrase or dependent clause is simply elided in Latin alphabet editions. For these reasons, I opted to translate the text from an early version in the Ottoman-Arabic script, in this case the 1923 edition published by the Orhaniye Press in Istanbul.[28]

In general, I have attempted to translate as many Sufi and Bektashi terms as possible. In cases where I have been unable to do so, or in which doing so would distort or impede the meaning, I have provided footnotes for explanation. In some cases, the novel itself explains the meaning of a technical term, so these have been left in the original as well. One particular word— *muhabbet*—deserves special mention as it is a central theme of the story and in Sufism more broadly. A term with a broad range of meanings originating from the Arabic term *muhabba*, *muhabbet* can mean love, affection, intimacy, and friendly conversation. As a technical term for the Bektashi order, it refers to a banquet or feast presided over by the shaykh at which the members of the order drink *rakı*—just as the Bektashi shaykh explained to Atatürk during their evening together at the presidential mansion—and sing hymns called *nefes* that Karaosmanoğlu called "the most distinctive Turkish music that exists." The author invokes *muhabbet* throughout the novel, nearly forty times, in various meanings: as a banquet, as an ethos, as an intimate relationship, as all-consuming passion, and as divine love. The novel also defines the term at different points. In order to retain the importance of this concept and its various resonances, it is one of the few terms that I have left untranslated.

In spelling proper names, I have retained their modern Turkish spelling, and the same approach has been taken for the neighborhoods and locations in Istanbul. Titles attached to names have presented another challenge. In the Turkish text, titles like *bacı* (sister), *hanım* (lady), *efendi* (gentleman/master), and *bey* (sir), appear with great frequency. My first renderings of the novel that retained all such titles made the text feel exceedingly formal and rather stilted, dashing hopes of a flowing text. As the frequency of such titles did not work well in translation, I have opted to retain them selectively, particularly when the title conveys an emphasis or special meaning. In most cases, I include the title at the first mention (e.g., Lady Nigâr), and subsequently provide only the name (Nigâr). For others, I retain the titles that clearly denote a special status or provide particular information about the character, so, for example, Nur Baba—the head of the lodge—is always Nur Baba, Dervish Çinari—the celibate dervish—remains Dervish Çinari, and the *grande dame*—Ziba—is always Madame Ziba, except when referred to otherwise. Admittedly, this is not a perfect solution and requires some degree of interpretation, but the act of translating hinges on such decisions and the alternative—retaining all titles—seemed less than desirable for the English language rendering.

---

28 Yakup Kadri [Karaosmanoğlu], *Nur Baba* (İstanbul: Orhaniye Matbaası, 1928).

Publishing a novel involving debauchery, substance abuse, and sexual promisicuity in a religious community is not a thing to be taken lightly. In making this rather polemical novel available in English for the first time, I very much hope that my aims are not misunderstood. It is worth stating openly that I do not endorse its negative portrayal of certain Bektashi leaders and communities, or of Sufi lodges more broadly. Hopefully, my Alevi and Bektashi colleagues and friends familiar with me and my work will attest to my sincerity in this regard. It is my aim that this translation will further discussion about religious stereotypes, Sufism, Orientalism, and gender within the secular-modernist zeitgeist of the early twentieth century, a context in which radical critique of religious institutions and leaders played a leading role and the marshaling of old, even ancient, religious libels for modern use captivated the reading public as well as the highest offices of state.

Nur Baba represents the transformation of Mediterreanean religious slander into modern national culture via the genre of the novel. It crystalized a derisive perspective on Bektashis, and by extension Alevis, that shaped the public discourse of both secularists and devout Sunni Muslims at the outset of the Turkish Republic. In general, Sufi lodges came to be seen as dens of perdition and Bektashis as deviant, though sometimes entertaining or charming, Muslims. The suppression of Sufi lodges and episodes of violence against Alevi-Bektashi communities in the Turkish Republic are but two manifestations related to these tendencies.

This early work of Yakup Kadri Karaosmanoğlu—one of Turkey's canonized national authors—is not only a rich primary source for various fields of inquiry but also a fascinating depiction of Istanbul, life in the grand mansions along the Bosphorus, and the elite society of the period. In addition to its academic importance for teaching and research, its value as a piece of literature is not to be underestimated. Aside from all the controversies surrounding the book, *Nur Baba* has flashes of brilliance. Its characters are memorable, and its plot reveals the quandaries of pursuing a spiritual quest in a modernizing society with deep social, economic, and intellectual divides. Set in the Ottoman capital, *Nur Baba* offers rich descriptions of the material culture, social dilemmas, and urban landscape of *fin de siècle* Istanbul throughout.

1 How Is the Candle Put out in a Bektashi Lodge?

"Is the alcohol finished?"

"For the master's sake, give us something to drink!"

"For the love of those who went thirsty at Karbala..."

"Our feast has dried up like a desert. One drop will give soul to the soul..."

"You misspoke. It's going to tie the *beloved* to one's own soul..."

"Both at once. By definition, 'one's own soul' means the 'be*loved's* soul.'"

"You poor rascal!"

"Hah, hah, hah..."

"O cupbearer, have mercy on us, come to our aid!"

"This old man needs help himself..."

"In that case, I command you: *Become wine!*"

"I did..."

"Enter the bottle..."

"No, look, I can't do that. I'd rather go somewhere else."

"Go into my mouth..."

"I don't want to, Sir..."

"Enter my heart..."

"What an *honor*. When God gives, *this* is how He gives."

On one of Istanbul's seven hills, in an old Bektashi lodge, a group of intoxicated disciples, men and women, greeted the dawn all talking together. The only one among them who didn't speak was Sister Celile, the wife of the spiritual guide. She listened to the drunken conversation with rage. Personally, she preferred not to overdo anything. Even more than her age, which was evident in the white strands on her head, it was the painful experiences of her life that had taught her the value of this rule. However, at this kind of banquet, no acquired wisdom was needed to see what distasteful consequences come from drinking sessions that carry on this long. Especially in this lodge, such an end was predictable because Nur Baba, the reckless young leader of the lodge, had no ability to control his disciples. Tonight, their nerves were stretched thin by the sound of hymns and songs, flutes and lutes, and hours of drinking. Most of the banquets he presided over ended disastrously with a brawl or a descent

DOI: 10.4324/9781003381471-2

into carnal pleasure. And so, Celile, still smoldering in anger, felt it necessary to stand up and sternly invite everyone to restrain themselves.

"By God, you've lost control of yourselves! Enough is *enough*. We've been drinking for eight hours. Daybreak is coming. Look, light is coming through the windows."

She turned to Nur Baba, who had fallen into a heated discussion with his disciple Madame Ziba. "*If you will command it,*" she said to him firmly, "we may go ahead and prepare the ritual meal…"[1]

Nur Baba answered with a half-angry, half-drunken smile, "Impossible, Celile. You can see that we still haven't shared our walnuts with Ziba. Of course if anyone wants to end the feast…" His final words were lost in a wave of protests. Everyone wanted to continue.

Sir Rauf and Lady Nasib, who had sat across from one another a bit earlier, were now right beside one another. Sitting Indian-style between the gentlemen Nesimi and Necati, the *oud*-player Niyazi began to tune his instrument again, for perhaps the twentieth time that night. As for Colonel Hamdi, who since the evening had made Celile's nieces writhe in laughter with all kinds of off-color jokes, he now completely devoted himself to clowning and contorting his face to embellish his puns and witticisms.

The heated conversation between Nur Baba and Madame Ziba was transforming into a genuine fight, inflamed anew with every glass. Giving up on her attempt to restore order, Celile sat back down, forcing herself to restrain her anger at the spectacle taking place before her. She turned to the cupbearer, who had been busy wiping the glasses without pause since the moment the *rakı* bottle had been finished.

"Nuriye, don't make me get up! Go find Dervish Çinari and have him fill up the bottle," she said. With a biting glare, she around looked at all those sitting in the room and mumbled to herself, "God forbid! What a lodge, what behavior!"

Nesimi heard this and leaned toward her, "Why are you upset again, Sister?" "For God's sake," she replied, "don't say that, sir. You of all people! You know what a lodge should be, and you know the rules of conduct better than me. Tell me, where have you seen a gathering or a ceremony like this? It's not at all clear when to eat or when the ceremony should conclude. Baba is enraptured. The children are doing whatever they want. There is no order, no discipline. Where is this going?"

"You're right, Sister. Tonight the ceremony really has gotten out of hand."

Celile drew her mouth toward his ear and indicated Madame Ziba with her gaze, "It's always this woman, Sir, always this woman!"

---

1 The term used here is "lokma," which literally means "morsel," but in Bektashi parlance refers to the consecrated food that is consumed at the ritualistic banquet known as *sofra*. See: Marc Soileau, "Spreading the Sofra: Sharing and Partaking in the Bektashi Ritual Meal," *History of Religions, 52* no. 1 (2012): 1–30.

Nesimi shook his head, half-protesting. "But no, Sister! It's really not fair to place all the blame on her. Look at the situation across from you: Lady Nasib and Rauf are practically on top of one another."

"After the master has set such a bad example, I excuse them."

Nesimi's eardrums felt the need to be rid of the young girls who ruined the flow of every round of songs and drinks with their continuous whispering, laughing, and flirting. And Nesimi especially wished to be rid of Hamdi.

"What do you say of this here Hamdi?" he asked. "Is it appropriate for him to be so involved with these young girls? Their reputation is well known, but, regardless, they are children, and their minds are immature. If you were to warn them once in a while, it would be a good deed. You don't know what kind of man this Hamdi is."

Nesimi's words gave Celile license to unleash the fury that was knotted up in her throat. She yelled at the girls in her most booming voice.

"My dear, what's the point of you being here? Tell me. You're good for nothing. You didn't tend the table or contribute anything to the party. And above all, you have been toying with poor Hamdi! How ill mannered, how despicable this is!"

Celile began to shout so loudly that Nur Baba and Madame Ziba appeared as if they might put an end to their conversation. Nur Baba sharply told his wife to be quiet. Ziba scanned her large, kohl-darkened, hazel eyes over Celile's white hair with a contemptuous glance.

Nasib leaned over to Rauf's ear while squeezing his knee under the table. "Everyone here is angry. A fight is about to erupt. Let's go and find ourselves a quiet corner somewhere," she whispered.

Rauf answered his lover's invitation with a naughty smile. "What's everyone else's fight to us, my dear? Is it so bad? While they bicker, we'll love." Rauf squeezed the young woman's hand in his palm.

Meanwhile, Necati leafed through the hymn book as the *oud*-player Niyazi strummed his pick lightly across the strings. The nerves of those present, worn thin by the uninterrupted eight-hour drinking session, slowly began to deteriorate with the symptoms of severe drunkenness. A profound fatigue overcame their eyes. But then Nuriye placed a replenished bottle in the middle of the table and Dervish Çinari began to refresh the *mezes*, which rekindled the nearly extinguished flame of the party.[2] As the first glass passed from hand to hand, from mouth to mouth, like a dim white flame, the gathering's initial vitality was completely revived. Nur Baba sang the first line of a Sufi hymn and soon the room's dispersed joviality united in harmony:

Before the Divine address "Be"[3]
at the beginning of creation were we.

---

2 *Meze* is a genre of small plates of food, often eaten together with *rakı*.
3 Reference to Qur'an 2:117, 16:40, 36:82, 40:68 in which God enacts his will merely by saying "Be!" and the act comes to pass, particularly with reference to the creative act.

Before anyone arrived to contemplation, O hearer
we were that "two-bow's length or nearer."[4]

Before the world knew Adam and Eve,
we were God with God in the dark mystery.
One night we stayed as Mary's guest,
we were the true father of the child Messiah blessed.

But they didn't finish the hymn, for suddenly, in the middle of the song, a voice called out.

"Enough already! My patience is finished! Have you no mercy, Master? By God, if you're going to continue, I don't care if it's the dead of night. I'll put on my scarf and get the hell out of here."

It was the voice of Madame Ziba. Nur Baba had continued to provoke her as the singing and drinking carried on. Now, everyone turned their eyes to him. He was dumbfounded, and quickly tried to make a joke of the situation to lighten the mood.

"Ah! Anything can come out of you, that's for sure. But I didn't expect you to be this brazen," he said.

Madame Ziba, who seemed to have shouldered the weight of her boisterous past fifty years while she sat, sprang from the floor with the quickness of a woman half her age and stormed off with such decisive steps that Nur Baba had to hold her by the skirt.

"I beg you, my lady," he said. "Let us settle our case in front of all the souls here."

Everyone accepted this suggestion with a sense of enthusiasm. Celile kept silent and looked straight ahead. Madame Ziba couldn't protest since everyone insisted, and so she sat in her place.

"My dear souls," Nur Baba began. "You probably noticed the heated, maybe even unpleasant, manner in which the Madame and I spoke just moments ago. We weren't speaking very discreetly because, in fact, I wanted to inform you all of the matter anyway. I am obliged to do so for various reasons. Don't think that I'm opening the subject on account of the lady wanting to leave. Oh no—there is nothing between us that needs to be kept secret. You can share in our conversation because the issue pertains to the lodge, to the public, and to you. This dear lady," he said, pointing to Madame Ziba, "despite being among the lodge's longest-standing members and despite the close friendship between us, has not visited us for some time now. This saddened us; however, we could not say anything. Coming or not coming was completely her decision. But the Madame did not stop at this. She became an impediment for those who want to come here, and she wished to turn her own house into a lodge, and thus put out the candle of the original lodge. For some time, I've

---

4 Reference to Qur'an 53:9 in which a majestic being, traditionally understood to be the angel Gabriel, approaches the Prophet Muhammad at a distance of "two bows' length or nearer."

heard that there is a young lady, a lady whom I have known since a young age, who wants to come here and take initiation. But the Madame, taking advantage of her close relationship to the lady, has dropped all she was doing and is using all possible means to make the poor thing abandon her idea."

Nur Baba said these words in a bitterly sarcastic tone. On his twitching, thin-lipped mouth, which his black, drooping moustache could not cover completely, there was a devilish smile. His eyebrows, linked by a thin line in the middle, crashed together; as for his eyes, they remained as lustful and listless as ever, preserving his perpetually enigmatic look. Everyone glanced around uncomfortably.

Madame Ziba rose up on her knees and said with a raspy voice, "The master is committing slander. Don't believe it! There is no lady who wants to come here. There is a young lady whom he would like to be brought here."

Then she went outside, moving at a speed that no one would dare try to stop. Nur Baba followed her for a moment with his eyes, and then leaned over toward his wife, whispered a few words in her ear, and Celile immediately walked out behind Madame Ziba.

Those seated asked one another secretly, "Who is this woman they're talking about?" Everyone wanted to know and asked each other in animated fashion, their eyes full of curiosity. The glances and whispers moved through the room—from Nuriye to Necati, from Nesimi to Niyazi, and from the young girls to Colonel Hamdi, who, taking advantage of the situation, had again surrounded him.

Only Nasib knew the truth. The secret passed from her lively, sensual mouth into the ear of Rauf: "It's Eşref Pasha's wife Nigâr..."

Nur Baba, in order to fill the silence, said to the cupbearer again and again, "Pour one more, Nuriye. *Pour!*"

However, by now, no one had the strength to drink. Morning had arrived. The first dim light of the dawn that had seemed frozen on the windows a bit earlier was now covering the entire room in brilliant whiteness. The forms that had been shaky and convoluted shadows by the light of the candles had now settled, and each gradually began to take on its real shape. The calligraphic scripts of the wall panels, which—as small rectangles on the wall—had appeared to be windows, could now be read, and the hangings on the large, rectangular stone they call "Balım Sultan" (after the famous mystic) no longer looked like strange, mangled tree branches.[5] The candles on the banquet table seemed like unnecessary decorations, their flames—shaking like thin white leaves of gold—shone and dimmed, dimmed and shone with a dull,

---

5 Balım Sultan (d. ca. 922/1516) was a foundational figure in the evolution of the Bektashi order. Removing him from his post in Thrace, Sultan Beyazit II appointed him to be the head of the Haji Bektash lodge and tomb complex in central Anatolia in 1501. Balım Sultan played a key role in the institutionalization of Bektashism as a formal Sufi order within the umbrella of the Ottoman system. He is remembered as the "Second Master" after Haji Bektash. See: Kara, *Grenzen überschreitende Derwische*, 58.

metallic flashing in the eyes of those sitting around. The faces around the banquet table resembled lithographic images. Nesimi's face was as pale as a sheet of paper, framed by his red beard. Beside him sat the *oud*-player Niyazi, who leaned against the back of his *oud*. Niyazi's plump eyes disappeared on top of his cheeks and the heaviness of a toothless old man's mouth replaced his youthful one. Necati was sitting nearby. Together with his wide, hanging mustache that covered half of his face, his face sagged and seemed to sink into his neck.

As for Colonel Hamdi, as soon as the young girls left him alone, he had left the banquet and then fallen asleep propped against the lodge's marble column. He appeared to be having trouble keeping his polished bald head on his shoulders, and it rolled right and left, front and back on his half-naked chest. Once in a while, it seemed as if he would collapse right onto Nur Baba, who was scratching the spot between his eyebrows with the tips of his fingers, eyes closed, face inert, in a state of idle irritability. Then at once he opened his eyes and nervously composed himself. Nasib's pink and plump body manifested a cheerful sensuality, sucking the sap of youth out of the man beside her, drop by drop. Next to her was another woman who sat still and directed her frighteningly fixed and strange gaze on the man with a black beard, Nur Baba, sitting opposite her. She was Nuriye, one of his old admirers and the cupbearer of the banquet. A heavy silence covered the room, like the steam in a Turkish bath. The candles melted slowly, drop by drop. Right then, Celile entered with Dervish Çinari behind her. On her face was the proud smile of someone who had resolved an important problem. She sat beside her husband in a dignified manner. Everyone turned their heads toward her.

Nur Baba leaned slowly to his wife and asked in a barely audible voice, "What did you do?"

She began to explain, jittering nervously. "Don't ask. Don't ask. Oh, the things I have endured. By the time I caught up with her, she had already put on her cloak. She entered the girls' rooms violently and kicked her servant awake. Her body was trembling with rage. I tried to speak to her, but it was as if she didn't hear me at all. Her servant began to dress herself and, being in the haze of sleep, didn't know what to do. I looked at Madame Ziba and thought: *This won't work.* So I said, 'The master sent me. He told me to make a request on his behalf.' This seemed to calm her a bit. She squatted on the cushion and began to cry. Then she fainted, and her hands and teeth locked up. Neither cologne nor the smelling salts had any effect. I had our girls and her servant undo her shawls, and I began to rub her chest. She came to a bit..."

"Get to the point! What happened?"

"You can't listen to the end of anything—'get to the point'—what to do with you! What do you think is happening? Now the servants are consoling Madame Ziba in her bedroom."

A deep thought overcame Nur Baba. He wished he hadn't angered Madame Ziba. Irritated, he rose to his feet and said, "I'm not going to eat anything. I'm going to bed right away. Help yourselves if you wish," and he left. Celile hurried behind him in a nervous state.

Rauf got up next. He too wished to sleep. Nasib ran to meet him in the hallway. The young lady said to her lover, "What if you stay a bit longer, Rauf? With the excuse of eating something, *please. Stay…*"

But Rauf excused himself in a manner that destroyed all of the lady's courage and walked straight to the northern door, the Door of Peace. Nasib stood for a while in the corridor, leaning against the glass that covered part of the meeting hall.

Inside, Dervish Çinari told jokes and everyone was laughing.

2 How Is a Bektashi Shaykh Raised?

Nur Baba regretted upsetting Madame Ziba. He lay upon his bed with his feet extended toward his wife. As she took off his socks, the night's events played like a nightmare through his groggy mind. He closed his eyes. Celile pampered his body with attention, but he stopped her.

"Celile," he said. "You must wake me up when she leaves!"

How many fights had he had with Madame Ziba—but who's counting? Tomorrow, as it had happened so many times before, everything would be forgotten, the argument would be blamed on too much alcohol, and the nervous, rebellious, powerful Madame Ziba of the previous night would again bend down and pay homage to him just like everyone else. Nothing so extraordinary or important had occurred in the conversation tonight that would prevent them from making peace as they had always done before. This was maybe the mildest of their fights, which they had been getting into frequently for the past ten years. There were even times when they had a half-serious, half-joking duel of words.

The next morning was the usual aftermath of a night of drunken revelry. After a long absence in a remote corner of the garden, Nur Baba and Madame Ziba emerged in a disheveled state—one's pajamas torn apart, the other's lace in disrepair—in front of everyone in the lodge. It seemed as if their love owed its strength and freshness in such fights and skirmishes and thrived in rage and anger. It seemed as if every crisis were a pretext to make them more connected, more indebted to each other.

In fact, it was true for only Nur Baba, for their arguments had left a nasty flame of resentment in Madame Ziba's heart. This flame always stoked up her grudge and drove her to seek concealed forms of revenge. Nur Baba could see the reflection of this flame in her eyes, but he hid his worries with a disarming smile. Anyway, which of life's events did not deserve a smile from a lazy-eyed dervish with a lustful mouth? He had seen the resolution of all his difficulties, perhaps even of all crises, in the world of wine and the reed flute, with a hymn or a few puns and winks. And at the beginning of every uphill battle in his life, he had always found hands extended to help him, arms carrying him, bodies spread on the ground beneath his feet like stairs. Since he was eighteen years old, he had been walking contentedly and peacefully toward his end

DOI: 10.4324/9781003381471-3

goal, which was pleasure, amid the sound of love, supplication, and passion. On his march, he was surrounded by a pious and melancholic procession of people prostrating themselves before him, women and men, young and old, crying out of love for him or sacrificing their souls on his path out of fear of him. Nevertheless, from within this crowd that elevated him to the status of a young god, there were only two individuals that left indelible impressions in the mind of Nur Baba. These two important figures had brought him to his station in life, and, once in a while, Nur Baba even felt gratitude toward them. His life was like a jubilant procession, with a sumptuous banquet at the front and a drum and flute ensemble at the rear. However, who knows on what precipice Nur Baba would have found himself, lonely and miserable, if he had been deprived even for a moment of the two gracious torchbearers who by turns cast light on his path with devoted fervor?

Because Nur Baba wasn't born as Nur Baba. Twenty-five years ago, he was the unknown, unwanted runt of the lodge which he now led, and the disciples then called him simply "Nuri." His predecessor, the late Afif Baba, had been denied the blessing of children, despite having been married four times. When he reached middle age, his inability to sire devastated him, and, when his last wife began to look at his face with eyes full of profound melancholy, the only way he could console himself was to take long trips. He wandered all over Asia, through Iran and Transoxiana. He stayed in Central Anatolia for two years, and it was there that he adopted Nuri and brought him back to Istanbul. At that time Nuri was eight or nine years old, puny and sickly, but very lovable and clever too. Everyone who looked into his eyes took a liking to them. Afif Baba liked him so much that even during the ceremonies he kept Nuri by his side. Eventually, this became the cause of complaints from disciples, the lodge's guests, and especially his wife Celile. And, despite the child's friendly disposition, he could be quite petulant when Afif Baba was absent. One night, in the midst of the Gathering Ceremony,[1] when things were at their most boisterous, Nuri called Baba over from his place and told him he was tired, and implored Baba to go to bed with him. When Baba opposed the child's whim, Nuri began to kick and shout furiously. This display was so distressing that afterward most of the guests began to distance themselves from Afif Baba's lodge, and those who remained reminisced about the gatherings of old.

By the time the child turned seventeen, almost no disciples remained in the lodge. The Nuri who before had only been troublesome and spoiled, was now aggressive and excessive with his first impulses of adolescence. There was not one female disciple, young or old, who had not felt, at least once, his hand roving over her thigh like a biting, thrusting, pinching animal under the table, or that had not experienced the beardless, scrawny youth throwing himself

---

1 The Gathering Ceremony or *ayin-i cem* is the name of the principle liturgical ceremony held by the Bektashi order, usually held on important occasions such as the initiation of a new disciple or the commemoration of a death, but also at other times depending on the traditions of a particular lodge.

upon their breasts in the corridor between the ladies' quarters and the meeting hall. The lad was unusually stubborn and persistent. Neither the slaps that descended upon his face, Afif Baba's warnings, the threats of other disciples, nor even the fact that his attempts were always met with harsh refusals, could impede his brazen behavior.

Indeed, Nuri resembled a young billy-goat in every sense. His unbearable behavior was becoming a source of confusion to the lambs of Haji Bektash's flock, whose comportment—down to the smallest mannerism—had been molded by the capable hands of their spiritual shepherds and whose conversations were marked by their charming refinement. Consequently, one by one, the sheep dispersed, and soon Nuri was alone in the great lodge. He suffered the first penalty of youthful inexperience, living in the empty lodge with Afif Baba dying in bed, groaning, and Celile bitterly plucking out white strands from her thick, chestnut hair every day.

However, not much time passed—only a year or two—before the bold and obstinate child found a way to rise triumphant. This path for him—since the day that Afif Baba fell on his deathbed—was through the bed of Celile, in a separate corner of the room, which he was able to enter only with great difficulty and danger. The young and passionate Nuri could not fully satisfy his lust in her mournful bed, but the relationship turned events in his favor. This relationship, which took on a formal and public character three months after Afif Baba took his last breath, attracted so much interest and curiosity that the lodge began to fill up again. The guests that had withdrawn, one by one, a few years ago returned in a flood to the exciting spectacle, and they brought the lodge unprecedented prosperity and wealth within a short period of time.

Curiosity is a great motivating force. The relationship between Nuri and Celile was so strange that it lured back the disciples that had drifted away. The disciples wondered—how could Celile venture to give a lawful form to such a moral failure, Celile who was known for being self-controlled, dignified, overly desirous of order, and even a bit puritanical among the disciples? How had Celile, who was approaching forty years of age, suddenly fallen into the embrace of a wild and reckless young man who had not yet hit twenty-three, a young man whom she herself had raised? No one thought that it was possible, and they surrounded the new couple with stunned looks on their faces.

Nevertheless, this couple didn't actually present such a strange sight. Afif Baba's young successor, with his face framed in a thick black beard grown prematurely, had long assumed the dignified look of a mature man, although his languid and sagacious eyes carried an allure of unrestrained sensuality. As for Celile, she had lost her composure completely, as if she'd been taken by a fever; her voice became as shaky as a young girl's, her cheeks were as red as a bride's, and her pale hair was dyed a brilliant color. As such, they looked quite fitting for one another. However, the old disciples could not forget that beneath the black beard of the man of today was the chin of the excessive, spoiled child of yesterday, and that in the golden hair of the young wife were the white strands of the widow of not so long ago. Seeing them side-by-side, these adepts could not overcome their sense of shock and dismay.

The newer disciples, however, viewed the young Sufi guide as a natural wonder. During the Gathering Ceremony, his mannerisms and movements—down to the smallest, most ordinary motions—appeared extraordinary to them. A single glance would provoke a thousand forms of analysis and myriad whispers. However, in regard to being a spiritual guide, Nuri Baba was no different from his predecessor. He appeared to be as knowledgeable of the Bektashi order's rules of conduct and the lodge's traditions as Afif Baba. One might even say that in this respect he was like a second copy of Afif Baba. He resembled the formal personality of the deceased guide. Nevertheless, there was the possibility that he could fall into error at any moment, due to his young age, inexperience, and ignorance. But Celile's loving hand was never far away; in fact, it rarely left the edge of his robe, always protecting him from making even the smallest error. Since the day she had lost her own will, her passionate sense of order could only be satisfied by controlling the will of others—particularly that of her young husband. Eventually, she held Nuri so tightly within her control that the youth began to struggle as if he had fallen into a spider's web. Yet every time he struggled, Celile would set him at ease with the smile of a compassionate mother and say, "For the peace of the lodge…" or "If the shepherd falls prey to his own whims, the entire flock goes astray."

For the peace of the lodge. This phrase usually subdued Nuri Baba, for he remembered the recent calamity of the lodge being completely empty. In Afif Baba's last days, Nuri had come to understand well what a deserted lodge was like, and he did not wish to have it empty again. But it was of no avail. His self-composure, which was artificial, did not last long, nor did the community's façade of orderliness.

One day, a woman named Madame Ziba from the Kanlıca neighborhood of Istanbul blew into the lodge in a perfumed and colorful gust and turned everything upside-down. This Madame Ziba belonged to one of the oldest and most renowned families of Istanbul. Her father was a rich and eloquent man by the name of Sir Safa, from the wine-imbibing, open-hearted, elegantly mannered men of the palace from the time of Sultan Abdülaziz.[2] He had a heart which was open to every lovely face and a stomach open to tasty food, just like his home was open to everyone, particularly to those with beautiful voices and eloquent words. Istanbulites over sixty years old call his

---

2 Sultan Abdülaziz (r. 1861–76) oversaw, for the first part of his reign, a continuation of the modernizing reforms of the Tanzimat. He was the first Ottoman Sultan to visit Western Europe and a member of the Mevlevi Sufi order. His reign took an authoritarian turn in 1871, and the economy deteriorated due to the accumulation of public debts, agricultural shortages, and sumptuous spending by the Sultan. Following the spread of revolts from Bosnia-Herzegovina to Bulgaria in 1876, his ministers deposed him, after which he died shortly thereafter, the official cause given being that of suicide.

Figure 2.1 Waterfront mansions on the Bosphorus at Kanlıca taken between 1903–1905. Somewhat lacking in paint, the Saffet Pasha Yalısı is visible, the second from the right.
Source: Anonymous, Courtesy of the Suna ve İnan Kıraç Vakfı Fotoğraf Koleksiyonu / Suna ve İnan Kıraç Foundation Photograph Collection, Catalog no: FKA 006263.

large home on the Bosphorus "Safa-abad"—the abode of Safa—in honor of Sir Safa.[3] This home, in the Bay of Kanlıca, with its windowed balconies, was once one of the most charming and enticing places on the Bosphorus Strait. Every night for the entire summer, laughter, the sounds of instruments, and cries of *"hey hey,"* whose brilliance never faded, poured forth ceaselessly from the luminous and open windows of the house, reaching all the way across the Bosphorus. The bay was full of lights and sounds, as if it were a festival. From both shores of the Bosphorus, starting from Bebek and Kandilli up to Sarıyer and Çubuklu, swarms of rowboats, swift and trembling, flocked to the bay in search of merriment and stopped at the grand house. Sometimes, those rowboats carried passengers from Beşiktaş and even Üsküdar. Even those heading to more serious destinations could not resist the desire to stop for at least five or ten minutes when passing by. Lovers who—under normal circumstances—could only yell to one another supplications for an

3 This is possibly an allusion to one of the most famous waterfront mansions of Kanlıca—the Saffet Paşa Yalısı—and its owner Saffet Mehmed Esad Paşa (1815–83).

encounter through poems recited from the opposite mansions across the water, now came slowly in their separate boats to talk side-by-side in the carnival of the bay.

The spectacle of the aquatic congregation never seemed to grow old, especially on moonlit nights, and Safa would endlessly gaze out the large windows of his balcony. The ladies' cloaks took on uniquely brilliant colors in the moonlight, and they seemed to Safa to be imaginary and transparent, made from light and water, standing in their rowboats as if they were hanging in a blue void atop the resplendent water. The groups of darkly clad men, who were always in the minority, wandered upon the gleaming surface of the water like fragments of clouds, indistinct and trembling.

Sometimes—on the nights when the moon was at its fullest—the crowd was so dense that it became difficult to separate the women from the men, and the men from the women. And sometimes those in the bay would join in with the revelry of those in the mansion—a round of songs outside could follow the one that had just finished inside and one of the listeners or spectators would complete the verse left half-finished by the singer. Sometimes it would happen that both sides sang the same song in unison.

On these boisterous nights, Safa did not take his hands off the large night-vision binoculars that he had brought back with him from his memorable trip to Paris—which he purported to use in order to identify the best singers in the bay—but in truth he wanted to see the faces of beautiful women. With his plump body on soft pillows and his elbows resting on the edge of the window, his eyes saw, searched, and daydreamed through the lenses of the binoculars for hours. He talked to those next to him, murmuring, like so,

"How sharp these binoculars are! Lady Hasene is standing right before me now…It's as if I could reach out my hand and hold her. In the boat right beside her is a gentleman that doesn't leave her alone for a moment. They look stuck together. Ha! The palace crowd has just come round the bend. God, what hairstyles…They're way past their prime…Hakkı Pasha's girls are opening up bit by bit…My oh my, look at Zeyrekli Nadire! She came right under our nose, but we didn't notice. She changed her rowboat, what grandeur! There now, there now, Faik's girls…How naughty they are! Day and night in the boat…I'll believe the gossip: there's definitely something going on between them and the boat boys. They speak to each other in such a familiar way and laugh together as if they were peers…That's strange…I can't seem to find the Egyptian Madame Raksınaz, perhaps she came and departed secretly?"

At this time, Safa's daughter was still very small. In the harem apartments at the back side of the mansion with her mother—who didn't like the noise—and her brother who never left her for a moment, she sat and listened to the echoes of the music that came from opposite directions, near and far. Sometimes she repeated the songs that she could hear clearly, in her cracked, tender voice, but she articulated them smoothly even though she did not understand their meanings.

When Safa Efendi was in a particularly cheerful mood, she would go up to the male quarters and listen to the singers up close, watching the festival of the bay on her father's knee through the balcony window. Naturally, the child understood very little from these sounds and the activity of the crowd, aside from a vague feeling of pleasure. Unfortunately, by the time she reached an age at which she could understand, the singers had gone silent, the bay had become deserted, and the balcony's wide window was shut. Since Abdülaziz's reign had come to an end in Istanbul, a completely different era had begun, and Safa had entered the ranks of those removed from their posts, put on pensions, and fallen from grace. Despite this, the great house of Safa, or "Safa-abad," had not lost its status as an attractive center on the Bosphorus. Safa's young daughter, the hazel-eyed Ziba, found another way to continue her father's night concerts and to attract passing rowboats into the bay. Her voice was as beautiful as her eyes. Her fingers were talented and as bewitching as her smile. After dinner, she would sit down in front of the piano and, once more, sweet music echoed off the opposite shore. She drew in droves of rowboats to the bay. The difference was that, this time, the rowboats deprived Sir Safa of the pleasure of his binoculars, because whether in moonlight or in darkness, Ziba was bringing in nothing but a colorless, drab fleet of men who remained pitch-black in the darkness, with only the tips of their cigars shining. The meaning of this drab hoard of men for young Ziba, whose hands moved over the piano and whose eyes roved around the bay, was immense. So much so that one day, this aquatic fleet rose up and pulled her out of the window of the mansion, like a mystical whirlpool, and, after this, wherever she was, young Ziba always remained inside this whirlpool.

The waves crashing against the shores of the Bosphorus circulated the story of Ziba among Istanbulites for three decades. Day and night, they roared the name of hazel-eyed Ziba, such that, over those three decades, there was almost no one who didn't know this name in Istanbul. Ziba deserved her renown, for she always did whatever was necessary to turn a small accident into an immense disaster or to transform a prosaic event into something legendary. She sacrificed the lives of her father, mother, and brother, the honor of her family, her youth, her beauty, her riches, everything, whatever there was, all of it. Nevertheless, all these things were not yet exhausted when she met Nur Baba. Her brother Sajit was living quietly in the mansion in Kanlıca, occupying himself with the education and grooming of his daughter Nigâr. Ziba herself still had a mane of light brown hair and had preserved her beauty and youthful appearance. Moreover, she lived a life of ease in the spacious mansion and its large garden, with a glamour that would make quite a few people envious, and her position in the dervish lodges was always right beside the Sufi masters.

However, none of these seats felt as lofty, comfortable and pleasurable as the one right beside Nur Baba. On the first night with him, she was so dazzled by his presence that toward the end of the ceremony, suddenly she knelt facing

Nur Baba as if she received a revelation, raised her hands to the sky as if in prayer and yelled wildly: "You are light! You are divine light, Nur Baba! Light, *liiiiight!*" With even more frantic, wild motions, she took the rings off her fingers and the earrings from her ears. She broke off the moneybag stitched with gold as well as the gold watch hanging by a thin chain from her neck and threw this handful of precious metal into the master's lap.

"From this moment on, let my soul, like my wealth, be a sacrifice for you and this exalted place," she shouted.

She bowed down and paid homage. From that night on, Nuri Baba came to be known as Nur Baba by all.[4] Nur Baba took the pile of precious metal that she had thrown into his lap and, with a very particular smile, placed it slowly in an empty *meze* dish on the table. Right beside him, Celile's agitated hand was pulling his robe, her elbow was prodding his, and she was using every possible facial expression to indicate to him that this inappropriate gift must be refused. However, as if he had drifted off in religious mediation, Nur Baba saw nothing, heard nothing, and his lips muttered words that only Celile would hear and understand.

"For the peace...and welfare of the lodge!"

Celile fainted upon hearing those words. From that night on, with only that single sentence, Nur Baba was able to force his level-headed wife to accept all the shenanigans of his relationship with Madame Ziba—which would last ten years—and to believe that the relationship was both natural and logical. However, there were quite a few disciples who found this relationship to be neither natural nor logical. They left the lodge one by one for reasons of jealousy or excessive piety. Indeed, the sincere Bektashis of old believed that it was a dangerous deviation for the spiritual guide to be obsessed with a single person, and therefore public romances were greeted with censure and abuse. However, the lodge of Nur Baba neither fell subject to any punishment nor did he feel the absence of those who left, for it was filling up quickly with the *bon vivant*, care-free group that had made the large halls of Madame Ziba's mansion reverberate with songs, instruments, and laughter. For some time, Nur Baba barely noticed the old disciples leaving or the new ones coming because Madame Ziba's love encompassed him like the sea. His eyes were immersed with only her color, his ears with only her voice. This pale-faced young spiritual master drank the complete essence of life from the wineglass of affection extended by his mature female disciple. From this glass, he imbibed—like the meaning of her name—the elegance of her gender.[5] From her presence, he learned the secrets of what Bektashi mystics call "*muhabbet,*" a combination of comradery and intimacy, both human and divine, that pervades the spirit and social life of the order. From her eyes, he learned the irresistible sorcery

---

4 The name Nuri means "belonging to light" or "covered in light," whereas Nur means light itself. The change in name here emphasizes the passage of the Sufi character from a boy to a man on the occasion of subduing and winning the devotion of Madame Ziba.

5 *Ziba*, a word of Persian origin, means "beautiful" or "elegant."

of the gaze that he now uses to make any woman silent. From her purse, he learned the pleasures that money provides.

What was Nur Baba before he met Madame Ziba? A mass of ambition, a heap of desire. Safa's hazel-eyed daughter Ziba melted this unpolished jewel in the fire of her breast. She sifted and filtered; she made out of him a hewn and meticulously cared-for idol, an idol of love, greed, and ambition. For this reason, Madame Ziba, who was now slowing with the yoke of fifty years and was now expected to seek pleasure and consolation in the watching the love of others like every older woman that sacrificed her life to *muhabbet*, continued to be jealous of Nur Baba. Against all odds, she wanted to conceal her final masterpiece.

3 How Is an Outsider Guided in?
Part I

The day after her fight with Nur Baba, Madame Ziba rushed to Nigâr's home. Boiling over with anxiety, she appeared on the young woman's door and immediately asked her:

"Nigâr, my dear, is it true that you want to become a Bektashi?"

This Nigâr was the daughter of Madame Ziba's late brother Sajit. Nigâr, along with her two children, had begun to reside with her mother in the waterfront mansion at Kanlıca, when her husband Eşref Pasha was appointed Ambassador in Madrid. For only the second time since her brother's death, Madame Ziba entered the mansion's door, which had remained closed to her for the past thirty years. However, this was not the second meeting in thirty years with her niece Nigâr. Even when her father was still alive and she remained completely under his control, Nigâr had secretly visited her outcast aunt. And, later, when Nigâr married and moved out of the mansion, the two of them began to meet openly. Blood ties and familial love were not the only forces pulling Nigâr toward her aunt, against the will of her entire family. Madame Ziba, with her life full of secrets and excitement, had always captivated her sensitive and dreamy niece. Ever since childhood, Nigâr had been enchanted by this strange life whose every dramatic, tragic event stood in sharp contrast with the calm house of her father. As she grew up, she began to see strong resemblances between Ziba and the great romantic heroines in the novels she read, and her heart was gradually filled with overwhelming amazement and admiration of her aunt. She saw Ziba's most basic, natural movements as extraordinary feats. And so, when Ziba suddenly came to her side in a state of anxiety that epitomized the meaning of the Turkish expression *"her skirt caught on fire"* and asked that unexpected question after closing the door behind her—"Nigâr, my dear, is it true that you want to become a Bektashi?"—Nigâr froze completely.

Madame Ziba tossed her purse onto a table, threw herself into an armchair, and, removing her gloves while her scarf was still on her head, continued:

"Don't just sit there! Answer me! This is *very* important…Yesterday all hell broke loose because of you! The lodge was topsy-turvy—there is nothing that I haven't suffered. Is it true that you have wanted to take initiation with the Bektashis for some time and that I've prevented you from doing so?"

DOI: 10.4324/9781003381471-4

Nigâr, shocked, said, "Aunt, what does taking initiation mean? Really, I don't know what you're talking about."

Madame Ziba's anxiety was gradually transforming into bitter anger. She continued talking, half to herself:

"So it was all slander! By my age, every possible type of slander has been made up about me. Even in this house...in this very room, inconceivably horrific stories, jokes, and intrigues have been invented about me, but none of them have irritated me as much as this last one: 'Nigâr wants to take initiation but her aunt Ziba is preventing this!' and, by implication, 'Ziba loves one of the Bektashi shaykhs, and for that reason she is jealous of her niece.' Slander this vile fills a person with hate."[1]

Madame Ziba's last words were full of caustic insinuations. Nigâr invited her to calm down, which made her aunt burst out in anger:

"Don't deny it, Nigâr! All gossip has some basis in truth. This much talk doesn't come from nowhere," she said. A strange shamefulness overcame Nigâr. She was like a child who was caught doing something wrong. She was investigating the reasons that may have brought about this first exciting event in her prim and quiet life. A moment later, laughing with a relieved smile, she said:

"Ah, now I remember. Just a moment ago, you said something about initiation—well, it just now came to me. I think all of this nonsense came from Nasib. She was here recently. First, as you can guess, she talked a lot about her Rauf. Then later, the conversation turned to the festivities at your lodge; she talked about it for hours. I listened and then, just to make conversation, I said: 'Ah, how much I would have liked to be together with you all, to be one of you...to see all of these festivities up close...' I hope that all these complications haven't come from one simple conversation!"

Madame Ziba finally took a deep breath, and while slowly removing her scarf, she said, "Don't doubt it at all, my girl." Her voice had softened dramatically. "Don't doubt this at all," she repeated. "Yes, from this simple conversation. Yes, from Nasib. This outrageous woman has turned Bektashism into a child's game. If it were only a game. She supposes that Sufi lodges are just places for meeting lovers. But the greater part of the offense is mine. All my mistakes come back to get me in the end. I'm not just saying this about Nasib. There are so many others as well. Ah, I thought they were decent people and assembled around the rug of a great spiritual guide, but but, alas, the rug of the master and these disciples are worlds apart. From the first night, they began to sing songs and shake their hips like dancing boys.[2] After drinking one glass too many, they went wild. If the guide looks at them once, it becomes impossible to restrain them. But, as we know, the guide's glance gives guidance; it does not corrupt. Drinking alcohol is fine, but not when it

---

1 Bektashis do not call their leaders *shaykh*s, but rather *babas* or *postnişin*s. Nevertheless, Yakup Kadri Karaosmanoğlu uses the term *shaykh* frequently to refer to Nur Baba.
2 This is a reference to "*köçek*," the male dancers who wear skirts and dance as entertainers.

causes dancing, hip gyrating, and finger snapping...*Drink is the cornerstone of the lodge.* At the very least, if only they could be discreet about what happens in the lodge! But no, instead they gossip, 'Was the lodge attended last night? Who went? What happened?' The following day these things circulate from mouth to mouth. But this is contrary to the foundations and spirit of the order! Why do they call it the Bektashi secret?[3] Because no one on the outside should know anything about what happens on the inside! The order's inner workings should remain secret. Isn't the entire sublimity and meaning of the order rooted in this principle? They suppose that Bektashism is easy; for twenty years I have been kneeling and bowing my head before the spiritual guides, but now if you were to ask me, 'What is Bektashism?' by God, I would be unable to give an answer. This thing that purifies the soul, that filters the essence and refines the gem in a person. So sublime, so deep...So..."

Madame Ziba's voice gradually took on a sad, soft, emotional tone.

"Now the ladies suppose that the lodges are just places for a rendezvous or lovemaking. Just seeing Rauf kiss Nasib gives one disgust of *muhabbet*, and love; they're exactly like animals, God forbid. But don't be offended. This generation, more accurately—your generation—is just as ignorant of love as it is of everything else."

Nigâr smiled and looked at the sea through the window. The water was calm and cool, with a ferry moving through it. Madame Ziba continued speaking for a while, with yawns interspersing her words. Gradually, she leaned her head against the back of the armchair with her eyes half-shut and said, "Oh God, how sleepless I am, how spent!" a few times in succession, and then went quiet.

Madame Ziba had fallen asleep. Nigâr wanted to pick her up and take her to bed, but she had fallen into such a sweet, deep sleep that Nigâr didn't want to disturb her. Sir Safa's granddaughter stood watching her aunt for a long time. The face that leaned against the armchair, from beneath a disheveled

---

3 The Bektashi secret or "Bektaşi sırrı" was a widely discussed topic in the last decades of the empire and the first of the republic. The late Ottoman public became fascinated, on and off, for several decades with the allegedly mysterious (and devious activities) of the Bektashi lodges. The idea that Bektashi rituals were arcane, sensual, heretical, and dangerous, crystallized into a shared fascination that was called the "Bektashi secret." Part fantasy, part urban legend, part religious bias, it fueled a great deal of discussion about Sufi orders, morality, and secrecy. Some scholars argue that the "Bektashi secret" developed over a longer period, namely, during the decades of clandestine existence of the Bektashis after the legal abolition of the Bektashi order in 1826. The Bektashi author Ahmed Rıfkı's book *Bektaşi Sırrı* (1909) tapped into this theme and was the first Bektashi work published after the fall of Sultan Abdülhamid II, see: Deniz Ali Gür, "Ahmed Rıfkı (1884–1935): A Francophone Bektashi in the Late Ottoman Empire" (Unpublished MA Thesis, Central European University, 2021). Aside from this larger public theme, the secret within the order refers to the esoteric knowledge transmitted only to initiates. See: Thierry Zarcone, *Secret et sociétés secrètes en Islam: Turquie, Iran et Asie centrale, XIXe–XXe siècles: franc-maçonnerie, carboneria et confréries soufies* (Milan: Archè 2002).

pile of colorful hair, was etched with lines, withered with immense fatigue: it looked like a colored veil that had stayed in water for too long. The edges of her eyes were puffed out and ringed by a dark, dull halo. Two deep lines that started at the sides of her nose and descended to her chin dragged the edges of her mouth downward and gave her entire face a disagreeable, depressing air. The young woman who stood observing was filled with a vague, trembling sadness. Nigâr pulled the curtains over the windows and tiptoed out, like a white shadow in the bleak darkness of the room.

Madame Ziba woke at dusk in a startled panic, opening her eyes and finding the room, which had been full of sun and sound just some time ago, now dark and deserted. She opened one of the curtains and looked outside: the sun was fading on the opposite hills. She realized that she had stayed too long; tonight she was supposed to meet Nur Baba at the mansion in Çamlıca in order to resolve the dispute from last night with a cool head.

She ran to the door and opened it, yelling "Nigâr! Nigâr!" Then she rushed to the mirror and began to put herself together. When Nigâr entered the room, she found her aunt with her headscarf and gloves on, and her bag in hand, ready to leave.

"Are you leaving? Why are you in such a panic, aunt?"

"Sweetie, we'll meet longer some other time. Tonight I have a number of guests coming to the mansion."

She kissed Nigâr farewell on the cheeks and, as she was walking toward the door, turned back as if something had just come to mind:

"Oh, I almost forgot," she said, "I was going to go to the bank today, but, of course, I didn't find the time. I won't be able to go tomorrow either. Could you give me thirty *lira* or so for the next few days?"[4]

Nigâr went to fetch thirty *lira* from her room, with her perpetual smile upon her lips. Madame Ziba, who got rid of two of her burdens on the same day, followed her, lively and carefree with nimble steps. In the wide hall of the mansion, at the top of the wide stairs, Madame Ziba, placing the money of her young and wealthy niece into her purse, with one foot on the stair, said to Nigâr in a slow and flattering voice, "My dear, tell me if you really do intend to join the order. These sorts of things should be kept hidden from the others. You're a married woman with children, you're young, you're inexperienced. Our path is not an easy one…Think about it. One also needs to be very self-sacrificing and willing to sacrifice all of this—wealth, comfort, everything…"

She couldn't complete the sentence and left briskly because Nigâr's mother was slowly climbing the steps, full of disdain and haughtiness toward Madame Ziba.

After her aunt left, Nigâr grew restless in the large rooms of the mansion as they filled with blood red light. She vaguely felt the urge to do something, but

---

4 *Lira* is a monetary unit.

this urge seemed hard to satisfy. It was as if Madame Ziba had taken all the meaning of the day with her and departed; the young woman wanted to give herself over to excitement, to agonize over gossip, to be libeled, to shout, to sleep, to go broke, to run and leave, to wait for visitors like her aunt was doing at that very moment. From the top of the stairs, she listened to the sounds and shouts of her children while they chased each other, as if it were the first time she had ever heard them. She went to the large window of the balcony, lifted the heavy glass pane and looked at the pink water of the inlet darkening with night. A rowboat drew near to the dock of the mansion and a tall, slim young man got out of the boat. He walked upon the dock's thin planks with confident steps, toward the mansion. This was one of her husband's relatives who came most nights to make conversation with Nigâr about literature, love, weather, freedom, and the lives of nations.

4 How Is an Outsider Guided in?
Part II

Not four days had passed when Nigâr received a message from her aunt:

> *My dearest Nigâr, we are expecting you tomorrow at the mansion. The issue*
> *we discussed has yet to be resolved; it persists and preoccupies us. Come and*
> *save me from this difficult situation in which I find myself. I cannot persuade*
> *them on my own, so your presence is necessary. When you leave the house,*
> *don't forget the possibility of staying the night at my place, so depart accord-*
> *ingly. I give you my warmest wishes. I'm definitely expecting you.*

Nigâr didn't fully understand the meaning of these words. Which issue? Who
are the ones expecting her? Friends of ours? Why is her presence necessary?
All of these things were unclear to her. Actually, the more she thought about
it, she was not completely at a loss as to what the unresolved issue might be
and could more or less guess who would be waiting for her. This was the rumor
about her wanting to become a Bektashi, the rumor that caused her aunt
to have black circles beneath her eyes, trembling nostrils, and fidgety hands
the other day. But for some reason Nigâr was not giving this the attention it
deserved. She was surprised that, with her name and one sentence alone, she
had caused such a fuss in a world where she herself was a complete stranger.
Nevertheless, she also felt a bizarre happiness at the same time. Several times
she said to herself: "These Bektashis are something else!" For a long time,
Nigâr had thought of them as outlandish and peculiar. Because of Madame
Ziba, Nigâr's father had, until the day he died, said every possible thing against
and told every unflattering story in existence about the Bektashis. When her
father talked about them, there was a particular expression that he used
which, even at a young age, shook Nigâr with hate and fear: "*Kızılbaşlar!*"
meaning Redheads, the followers of the Shiite Shah Ismail.[1] For her, this word

1 The term Kızılbaş or "red head" refers to the red-colored head gear worn by the disciples
of Shah Ismail (1487–1524), the Safavid Shah, who came to embody the threatening specter
of Shiism. His Turkish-language poetry is still widely enjoyed and revered in contemporary
Turkey, particularly among Alevi and Bektashi communities. The Ottoman state called the
Anatolian followers of Shah Ismail "Kızılbaş" in a derogatory manner, and the term has a

DOI: 10.4324/9781003381471-5

was replete with nefarious meanings similar to those associated with "witch," "zombie," and the like.

A rather intelligent and enlightened woman with two children, Nigâr was approaching thirty years of age. However, the fear instilled in her by this expression during her childhood persisted; "Kızılbaş" still came to her mind when someone said "Bektashi," and her whole body shuddered with a fear mixed with hatred. One effect of this childish reflex was that, despite all of Nigâr's curiosity and desire, Madame Ziba's adventurous, exotic dervish milieu remained beyond the pale to her. Her aunt's life was a book whose every page contained a different legend, but the one episode Nigâr did not understand at all and found strange, even a little vulgar, was her escapade as a dervish over the past decade. Nigâr could not fathom how this spirit, who grew up around the most refined music, the most eloquent lyrics, the most elegant forms and people, this woman who inspired one of the greatest poets of her homeland to write poems of outstanding beauty, could one day fall into the arms of a dervish wearing baggy pants and a coarse belt around his waist.[2] She could not comprehend how she poured out the essence of her ego—to the very last drop—upon the mysterious ground called a Bektashi lodge. Nigâr found her descent down this path worthless, meaningless, and lifeless. For that reason, she became curious, if nothing else, to see the dangerous threshold of that dark assembly that could bring down the extravagant Madame Ziba, in all her pomp and splendor, to her knees.

Recently, a young woman by the name of Nasib, who had just passed through this threshold, gave Nigâr the particulars about the Bektashi gathering; however, all these details only intensified the curiosity in Nigâr. Because Nasib viewed Haji Bektash's hearth as the most appropriate place to come together with her lover Rauf, she described lodges in a manner completely different than Nigâr had imagined them. If one were to rely completely on Nasib's description, it would seem that a Bektashi ceremony resembled the debauched orgies of Nero, Petronius, or Trimalchio.[3] For that reason, Nigâr's curiosity was piqued, and one day she said with total sincerity: "Oh, how much I would have liked to be there together with you all!" However, this desire never for a moment transformed into intention because her nature lacked determination and courage; it vacillated, always remaining in a dormant state.

In addition to surprising her a little, angering her a little, as well as making her a bit happy, her aunt's message that morning amplified that speck of desire

---

wide range of connotations in Turkish, mostly negative. In many dictionaries, *kızılbaş* is listed as meaning "incest."

2 *Shalvar* (*şalvar*) is a type of baggy pants associated with rural life.

3 Nero, the infamous Roman Emperor, reigned 50–54 BCE. Petronius or Gaius Petronius Arbiter (d. 66 CE) was a Roman statesman in Nero's inner circle and is believed to be the author of the *Satyricon*, a satirical work that portrays Trimalchio as a vulgar but extremely wealthy freedman who entertains his guests at an obscenely extravagant and distastefully lavish banquet.

sleeping in a corner of her heart. She knew that the place she would go, her aunt's mansion, was not a Bektashi lodge, but it was definitely something akin to one.

The following day she swiftly accepted the invitation. She was only able to reach her aunt's mansion toward the evening, since, as usual, she woke up quite late in the morning and was slow in getting herself ready and getting out of the house. Those at the mansion had lost hope that she would come and drifted off into their own particular worlds. Nigâr found them half-drunk around a large table on the mansion's wide balcony. The table was covered with a white tablecloth, bottles, drinking glasses, ice, and *mezes*. At first glance, the scene intimidated her so much that she thought about turning back, despite the eagerness and courtesy that were being shown toward her by everyone. However, her heart, which was as soft as her body, feared offending her aunt, and she loathed the thought of appearing timid and immature in front of those present. She greeted everybody one by one with the elegant, pleasant smile that always adorned her face.

Around the table were three women and three men, including Madame Ziba and Nur Baba. The other two women were Celile and Nasib, and the other men were the *oud*-player Niyazi and Necati. Nigâr sat down in a wicker armchair beside Nasib and, appearing to fall into a lively discussion with her, actually began to analyze those around her with furtive but piercing glances. The man said to be Nur Baba exceeded both her expectations and imagination: he was not wearing baggy pants, nor was there a belt on his waist; he wore a white linen vest with a closed collar, a pair of dark pants and, in place of a coarse wool cloak, a robe made of fine black cloth. This clothing had a simple, elegant dignity that suited him well. Only his head looked disorderly, even slovenly, atop his tidy clothing. His hair was utterly disheveled, and his bangs hung down over his eyes. His beard was too long, and appeared as if he had never combed it; his face was pale, and his eyes were so languid that they seemed liquid. In her mind, Nigâr likened this face to a charcoal portrait of Jesus' disciples, especially to a young Saint John.

She didn't dwell long on the others. However, she examined Celile with particular care and quietly asked Nasib, "Is this white-haired woman the shaykh's wife…? She's so old!" While she said this, Nigâr sensed that Nur Baba had leaned over and whispered a few words about her to her aunt. She didn't need to wonder for long about what he'd said, because Madame Ziba conveyed the guide's words to her:

"His Holiness is asking if you wouldn't like to drink something?" Nigâr refused. She didn't even know what *rakı* tasted like. At most, she could have maybe a few glasses of beer at a meal.

After this Nur Baba said directly to her:

"Madame, if it's going to be that way, you're going to be very bored among us! In our opinion, the source of the conversation, gaiety, and camaraderie at this very moment, is the liquid in this bottle. We extract the wisdom of speech from this, we derive the eagerness of our spirit; in its throes we know, understand, see, and love one another."

Nigâr was smiling as she listened. Necati interrupted the speech:

"So true, Your Holiness," he said. "Your words are full of light"—and he read a few lines from the old manuals of the cupbearers, turned to Nigâr, and added these words with an air of consummate wisdom—"The Westerners did not deny the spiritual properties in this blessed water, and they called it 'The Water of Life,' isn't that so, Sir?"[4]

"Indeed so, my dear man," Nur Baba said, cutting short Necati's monologue, and then addressing Nigâr, "Until the end of this evening's *muhabbet*, we will yearn for you, and you will remain a stranger to us. Clearly you possess a very perceptive heart and intellect—the hidden meaning beneath our speech and mannerisms cannot remain secret to you...but we wanted you to be completely one of us. Let your brilliance join in the congress of enlightened souls."

While saying these words, he extended his own half-full glass to Nigâr in a manner particular to the order. The young woman became uncomfortable and blushed. She wanted to excuse herself, but it wasn't possible. All of a sudden, everyone was insisting, and beside her Nasib said anxiously:

"Oh goodness, don't refuse! The guide is giving you a drink with his own hand and his own glass! This grace isn't offered to everyone, what are you doing? Be careful!"

Nigâr took the glass, brought it to her lips but without taking a sip, and set it back on the table before her. Nur Baba said to Madame Ziba with an enigmatic smile:

"Your niece has both trampled on your destiny and wants to impede mine, how cruel!"

Nigâr could not understand the meaning of this snappy remark, and she looked at her aunt and then at Nur Baba's face; thankfully, Celile came to her aid from the opposite side of the room:

"Madame," she said. "Actually, because you are an outsider, you're not obliged to follow our rules; however, it never hurts to learn something new. In our view, the drink given by the guide cannot be refused. It should definitely be accepted, and one must drink it to the last drop and then return the glass to him."

Nigâr let out a forced laugh and said:

"What an elaborate ceremony, really!"

---

4 The *sakiname* is a genre of versified literature that deals with the etiquette for cupbearers at gatherings with alcoholic drinks, as well as the rules, the music instruments, and the food these parties entail. A good example of an Ottoman *sakiname* is the *İşretnâme* of Edirneli Revânî (d. 930/1524). Some *sakiname* use the terminology of wine to engage in mystical discourses within the Sufi tradition, an early example of which is Kalkandelenli Fakîrî's *Sâkînâme*. Famous poets and writers from Fuzûlî to Namık Kemal composed in this genre, and such works continued to be written into the twentieth century, the last specimen of which is thought to be that of Mehmed Memduh Pasha. See: *Türk Diyanet Vakfı İslâm Ansiklopedisi*, "Sâkînâme."

She extended the glass that had touched her lips to Nur Baba; the young shaykh with the unkempt beard leaned over from where he was sitting, placed one hand on his chest, and, in one gulp, drank all the contents of the glass.

Following this, Nigâr saw the same glass filled and handed to her aunt by Nur Baba. The others were emptying a different glass in turns, which was filled and passed out by Celile. The young woman found this ceremony disgusting and vulgar; in particular, the coarseness of the spiritual guide's efforts to assign immense value to his own glass seemed excessive to her. She leaned over to Nasib, who was subjected to the awful degradation of finally emptying the glass that had passed from mouth to mouth because she was the newest of the disciples. Laughing, Nigâr said:

"Being a Bektashi *really is* difficult…"

These words somehow the caught the ear of Nur Baba who was reaching toward a *meze* plate in front of Nigâr. Holding a large olive on the end of a fork, he turned to the young woman and said:

"My lady, it's not that difficult; one must only separate from pride and conceit, and from the importance of anything besides God."

Though she did not completely understand this last sentence of Nur Baba's, Nigâr felt the need to respond and attempted to explain herself. However, right at this moment, her aunt's deep voice called out to her through one of the mansion's windows: Madame Ziba had gone inside suddenly just a moment before. This saved the young woman from the tight spot she was in, and she went running in the direction of the voice. A moment later a servant approached Nur Baba with an invitation, "They're waiting for you inside as well," and he followed them inside behind the servant.

Those remaining at the table looked at one another with telling glances. Celile said, "This is to resolve that problem from the other night."

Actually, Madame Ziba, who, in her own mind, had elevated the problem to the level of a trial on her self-respect, had not been able to sit still since her niece had arrived. Now she wanted to correct the general impression that she had degraded into a jealous and aging disciple who was fearful of being abandoned and thus strove to fend off the younger women who wanted to get closer to the guide. At the same time, across from the young master who appeared so proud and full of self-love, Madame Ziba had the desire to behave in a carefree way, no matter what, and if it were possible, to push Nigâr into his arms with her own hands. She knew this would be a heart-rending revenge for both Nur Baba and herself. However, in bringing down a crushing blow upon this gradually fading, final *muhabbet*, this aging, passionate priestess of love was even now experiencing rabid pleasure. With her own hands, she was burning down the ten-year palace of pleasure that she had built with her own hands, through a thousand hardships and at the cost of her soul and wealth. Without a doubt, the eyes of friends and enemies alike would be dazzled before a fire like this, by this display of her power.

Madame Ziba had taken her first step toward this goal by inviting Nigâr to the mansion tonight and having her meet with Nur Baba. This action of hers shocked all the disciples who knew something about the situation. Even Nur Baba was rather surprised when he was called inside. Both aunt and niece were waiting for him in the salon of the mansion.

Madame Ziba said with a cold, out-of-place smile:

"Right this way, your holiness; really, we've committed a shameless act calling you to our presence. However, this is for what is, in your view, a matter to be resolved." Nur Baba had no idea what she was going to say. Madame Ziba continued:

"Will you please ask Nigâr? When and how have I wanted to impede her wishes and actions?"

The scraggly bearded guide laughed and said:

"Is this a court room?"

He turned to Nigâr:

"Let's see. Madame, would you permit me to ask you a question like this?"

The young woman found the situation unbearable; her ever-present smile vanished, and the paleness of anger had come to her always-rosy face. She said these words in a sudden attack:

"Sir, I have unknowingly given cause to a misunderstanding between my aunt and yourself; an unimportant comment of mine has been exaggerated, and a problem has arisen from this. My aunt did not have an inkling of an idea about this; even I know nothing about it."

Nur Baba didn't know what to say; Madame Ziba flew out of her seat.

"Did you hear, Your Holiness?" she said and placed herself right next to the spiritual master. With a slow, begging voice, she said, "I hope that you are magnanimous enough to give a proper explanation to those sitting outside."

As she said this, she walked toward the door as if she were dancing.

"Now, I have been relieved of all blame," she said. "I'll leave you two alone. Converse as you wish!"

She left quickly, warbling with the sauciness of a young girl.

Nigâr couldn't make any sense out of this last antic of her aunt. She sat there, frozen. The unkempt-bearded shaykh was standing and he appeared to have forgotten what he was going to do or say. The room, whose windows were covered with ivy, had filled with the shadows of night. The veins in Nigâr's temples were throbbing and her head was aching; her whole body was tingling from a current of energy emanating from the man across from her. She felt that she had been left alone and helpless in the presence of immense danger. She stood up and said with a trembling voice:

"Let's go outside, Sir."

They walked, Nigâr in front, Nur Baba behind, down a long luminous corridor that led to the balcony. A servant passed them, carrying a tray full of dirty plates in his hand, and he gave them a knowing look. The master said to the young woman:

"The truth is that your aunt's a real pistol."

The young woman did not respond; for reasons that cannot be known, she hurt both for herself and for the one at her side, and her heart was filling slowly with hatred toward her aunt. When they came to the threshold of the door that opened onto the corridor's wide view, Nur Baba cried out:

"God, what a sublime sunset!"

Nigâr looked at the hills whose trees had turned pink, the shadowy forests on the slopes, the distant sea, and the red horizons. Moda Burnu, the Fenerbahçe Lighthouse, and the Princes' Islands could be seen from here. The sunset was so fluid and rich with color that it seemed to be a fantasy. The scraggly-bearded dervish showed another side of the horizon to the young woman with a broad motion of his arm, saying:

"Look over there as well!"

A large, round, copper-colored moon was coming up over the top of the Kayışdağı hill.[5] The young woman looked at all of this with unseeing, clouded eyes. At this moment, she felt that she was far from everything and everyone—forgetting, forgotten, thrown into another world.

They found those at the table full of mirth, singing songs and playing the *oud, tambur,* and *def.*[6] Madame Ziba was merrier than everyone else, tipsy as usual. As Nur Baba entered, they all quickly stood up to show respect to their master. Celile straightened out the cushions and pillows in the armchair for her husband to sit upon, and Nigâr saw the despicable and pathetic man from a moment ago settle into the armchair in a rather imposing manner. Nur Baba made a commanding gesture that announced to Madame Ziba that he wished for her to fill his glass. Nigâr was astounded by how fast everything was forgotten in this bizarre world; the unbearable scene from just minutes before had left no trace upon the faces of either Nur Baba or Madame Ziba. She, on the other hand, was still shaken, even though she was more or less a spectator beholding this drama.

She wanted to get away from this place right away, even if only for an instant. She said to Nasib, who was, for whatever reason, sulking by the corner of the table:

"My dear, Nasib, would you accompany me? I want to stroll around the garden for a bit."

Nasib accepted right away. A bit later, the two young women were talking side by side in the far end of the vast dilapidated garden.

"You created a mess for me, Nasib, an impossible mess! What got into you, to let loose a rumor like this based on nothing? It's true that I told you that I'd like to be a Bektashi, but I just said that to make conversation. I should speak more carefully with you from now on. Oh, Nasib, you can't imagine the drama that I'm going through! Moments ago, I was needlessly thrown into no-man's-land, into a despicable situation; I became the target of defamation.

---

5 Kayışdağı is a hill of 438m located on the Asian side of Istanbul in today's Ataşehir district.

6 The *tambur* (or *tanbur*) is a type of stringed instrument widespread in Iran, Central Asia, the Caucasus, Mesopotamia, and the northeastern Mediterranean. The Turkish version has a long, thin neck and three pairs of strings. The *def* (or *tef*) is a light animal skin drum, similar to but larger than a tambourine, usually pulled over a wooden frame.

Will you at least recognize that all of this is because of you, because of your exaggeration?"

"Don't falsely accuse me, Nigâr! By God, I am not the cause. The inclination that Nur Baba feels toward you, together with your aunt's crazed jealousy, have caused this crisis, not me."

"What are you saying, Nasib, my dear?"

"I'm telling you what I've seen, heard, and know, Nigâr. There's no other way to say it: Nur Baba loves you. He ran into you one day, I don't know where, when you were out with your aunt. Your veil was open and he saw your face. From that day on, he talked of nothing but you. One time when we were alone, he was drunk, burning with love, and opened up to me. When he pronounced your name, by God, every hair on his face trembled, one by one. So I said: 'Don't worry. One day you will realize the bliss of seeing her among your children. Because Nigâr has the desire to take initiation.' This is what I said. The news went straight to Madame Ziba, and attempt after attempt was made to contact you but none of them succeeded. Your aunt even stopped coming by the lodge. She was preventing and opposing you from joining the order in every possible way. So, for no reason at all we got into this mess."

"How strange…but by what right is your shaykh coming after me? It seems that everyone here has really spoiled him."

"Don't talk like that, Nigâr. There are many among us who are ready to sacrifice our lives for his path. And besides, masters cannot be unloved. For instance, there was a poor woman by the name of Madame Ülker who threw herself from the window of the lodge after he mistreated her one night. She wanted to commit suicide. Now she sits in her house with two paralyzed legs."

"What are you saying, Nasib? For this guy she jumped out the window?"

"Don't underestimate 'this guy'! He is completely love, completely fire. If you look carefully into his eyes just once, you will feel that you have melted. His heart is quite aloof; however, when he loves, he loves dreadfully. You know that I'm quite impartial in this matter. Nothing has ever occurred between the two of us. I am already overwhelmed by Rauf…well, despite this, I'll say it plainly, that if Nur Baba wanted to…"

"Nasib, you can't be serious!"

"Oh, I'm telling the truth, sister! Whatever I am on the inside, I'm the same on the outside! I don't enjoy hypocrisy, lies, or secretive dealings. Unlike your aunt."

"Oh heavens, don't mention her."

"On the contrary, I think she's precisely what we should talk about because I see that you still have no idea what kind of material your aunt is made of. Learn and behave accordingly hereafter. I have never seen another woman in the world who lives with as much cheating and lying as this one. To cover up one lie, she tells another; to cover up for cheating, she cheats again. Pay attention, everything is for show. She lives for show, she loves for show; her crying, her laughing, everything is a performance. Today, her calling you here, leaving you and Baba alone in a room. All of this, in order to appear humble, noble, and brave in front of everyone. Among her other activities today, she also did me wrong. Allegedly, Rauf was going to be here tonight. That's what she said when she invited me; now she's saying, 'I sent word, but he didn't come.' By God, it's a lie! No one sent word, nor did anyone say 'I can't come.' She did this to irritate me. She's knows that I have a violent need to devote myself to Rauf when I'm away from my husband. And, God bless her, she has yet another nasty habit: she cannot stand for people around her to be in love. She is jealous of everyone and anyone; she wants the whole world to be occupied with her, with Madame Ziba. Is that possible?! Her face has turned into a rotten peach, not that she doesn't realize this herself. This is why she always resents young people. For instance, you, Nigâr, she can't bear you at all."

"But, what could have I done to her? I don't even see her often."

"God protect us, how much worse it would have been if you'd actually done something! Listen, if I gather together what I've heard with my own ears the things she said about you to Baba, it would make up a thousand-page book of libel. Allegedly, there is no other woman on earth as messy and shiftless as you. Apparently, you're young and gorgeous, but what good is it, she says, to have such a sublime vessel, if within it there is an icy heart. Reportedly, even your husband grew tired of this cold nature of yours and escaped to distant places. There's more: allegedly, there is a relative of yours, a young man by the name of Macid, whom you have been in love with and trying to get in your clutches for years, but you have been unsuccessful. You even spent quite a sum of money on that youth, and you wouldn't leave his side for a minute, such that he became sick to death of you... ."

"How strange. Anyway, there's a contradiction in this. Seeing that my heart is like ice, how could it be that I loved Macid with such fervor?"

"That's why Nur Baba is laughing under his mustache at all of this! Oh, if I were in your shoes, Nigâr..."

The evening's flowing pinkness had departed; in its place shone the moon's pale light. Even from a distance, the sea was brilliant and calm like a large enchanted mirror. The garden was silent. Suddenly a deep, melodic, sad voice surrounded the two young women like the sea on a silent night and left them trembling. It sounded like the lament of the setting sun. Nasib said slowly:

"Nur Baba is singing."

In the opinion of the disciples, Nur Baba's voice was as irresistible as his eyes. Nigâr, too, was entranced by this voice, from the very first note. This was a strong, unusual, and impressive voice, like the roar of natural elements: it was the sea, it was the wind, the hum of the forest, the peal of a wave, the light play of water. The music touched the deepest depths of their souls, and they listened for a long time. Nur Baba sang:

O, wild gazelle, don't run from your lover, come, be intimate
Don't be a stranger, come, be loyal

Come to the banquet, make your parting drunkenness into the joy of reunion
Sing, rise, dance, pour drinks, converse.

After his voice ceased, the two women stayed for a while longer, in a state of amazement. Nasib gave a saucy, sensual laugh, and said to her friend, "Did you hear? This is all for you. No matter how much the others beg, he doesn't condescend to open his mouth and sing a single verse. But for you, he pulls out all the stops! Oh, with what burning passion he loves!"

Nigâr replied, "I don't know about his eyes, but his voice is disastrously good."

Now they could hear Niyazi's improvisations on the *oud*. Nigâr and Nasib stood and gradually made their way back to the mansion.

Nigâr had become enlivened with the music. As she walked, it seemed as if she were dancing. No trace remained in her body of the headache and the awful chills from a bit earlier. When she arrived in front of the people sitting on the balcony, she was as merry as Nasib.

From where did this mirth come? There was nothing that had changed in these last regrettable three or four hours since she had been at the mansion. It was a continuation of her being left alone in an empty room with a strange and aggressive man, of her name roving around in the mouths of drunkards, of being a defenseless, lone woman who had come to the house of an old hussy in order to put to rest a number of vulgar rumors. Nigâr sat in the armchair on the balcony, and for a moment left herself to these thoughts and impressions. The music had quieted down. Nur Baba and Madame Ziba were speaking insinuating and perplexing words, and everyone tried to eavesdrop. Every once in a while, Celile wanted to intervene, but she did not. Necati was laughing continuously. Niyazi's eyelids had become heavy, and he was engrossed in one of the *mezes* in front of him. Nasib signaled with her eyes at Madame Ziba and said secretively to Nigâr:

"What do you think of that? It seems as if the woman has her prey in hand yet again."

Madame Ziba sensed that there was a conversation going on about her between the two young women and said with a half-drunken laugh:

"Nigâr, the truth is that today you really made me despair. His Holiness says that it's not possible to guide you."

The young woman looked awestruck at her aunt, as if she hadn't understood the meaning of this quip. But Nur Baba said immediately with sincere anger:

"Your aunt is lying. Since I already know that you won't rely on her words, I'm not going to get into expositions or explanations." He planted his angry, scolding eyes on Madame Ziba.

This intervention of Nur Baba pleased Nigâr. In her heart, she even felt a bit grateful toward him. She turned her beautiful face with its gentle smile toward the spiritual guide. The moonlight's reflection had given her face a sweet paleness. Nur Baba looked at her in adoration.

At this juncture, Mother Celile, who considered it her duty to bring order to gatherings that had gone off track by such glances or words, said repeatedly:

"For goodness' sake, let's sing a song. Just one song so we can all collect ourselves, and Nigâr will have had the experience of hearing it."

Despite this, a half-disgruntled, half-murmuring, and pregnant silence loomed over the group for some time. At last, Nur Baba began to sing, and, they joined him all at once. There was wonderful enthusiasm in their voices. Nigâr listened carefully: it was a mystical and lyrical hymn made up of quatrains. The young woman had never heard a song of worship so enthusiastic, such that when they went quiet, she requested that they sing the piece again. They repeated it with even greater feeling. After this, Nur Baba requested two things of Nigâr: one, that he might give her a glass of *rakı* with his own hand; the other, to drink a drop of *rakı* from the glass that she might give to him.

The young woman gave a wry smile at the supplication of the Sufi master with the disheveled beard. Madame Ziba laughed wildly and shouted to Nur Baba:

"You're finally succeeding in bringing her under your guidance. After all, she's still of my blood…"

Nigâr went to bed early but couldn't sleep till the morning because the voices of those on the balcony could be heard on the top floor of the mansion. After the voices ceased, she leaned against the window for a spell. She watched the moon roll gradually toward the sea like a bloody head in a corner of the horizon, and she listened to a Scops owl's short, successive hoots. The dawn was fragrant and cool.

5 Two White Moths Circling around Haji Bektash's Candle

"What day is today, Macid?"

"Today? I don't really know either. I think it's Friday. The days look so much alike that it doesn't seem necessary to give them different names."

"The months and the years feel like that too, Macid."

"It's like that for me but, I don't know, is it like that for you as well? Your husband went to Madrid last year. Two years ago, you brought a child into the world. Five years ago, you had another child. Before that you were engaged, wed, and married."

"Ah, I barely remember when those events happened or how they felt."

"That means that you've been very absent-minded, oblivious to the world even. You've lived with unseeing eyes and deaf ears."

"No, Macid. I have seen and heard. However, the truth is that I found neither what I've seen nor what I've heard to be worthy of attention…I've forgotten everything from my past."

"Don't say that, Nigâr Abla. I know that your soul is like a bird with its head tucked under its wing. You stay closed off, hidden from the outside, and, in the name of life, you listen only to the beating of your own heart. If you were to open up a bit, to stir, to fly…"

"Quiet, Macid, quiet. You don't know. Living is a very difficult business, a very dangerous art. It is practically acrobatics, learning to look from above, to use the tightrope walker's pole, to walk on a thin wire, not to fear falling. In short, one needs to have quite a few talents and a great deal of courage."

"You speak as if you've had some experience in this, Nigâr Abla!"

"Experience? Yes, that isn't difficult to acquire. It suffices to see those who really live up close. But I didn't stop at that. I breathed in the air of an entourage that is like a fire burning with the colorful flames of a thousand desires. This air was painful and full of scents that made my head spin. The truth is that I prefer the dimness of my room to that foggy enlightenment."

"You're a pale and timid moth, Nigâr Abla!"

"You're like that too, aren't you, Macid?"

"Me? If you only knew how much and how profoundly I've lived…Well, actually, no one has heard my voice. I'm like a strange shadow, but I'm as full of experiences and great events as a nation's history. If anyone were to see my

DOI: 10.4324/9781003381471-6

inner life, what disasters, what joys, what adventures they would see. I'm not timid and innocent, Nigâr Abla, but tired and drained."

"Have you ever loved, Macid?"

"..."

The dark-haired young man looked at the horizon with unsettled eyes. The day had suddenly become bright yellow behind the hills on the other side; the air, dead still. Macid lowered his eyes to the bay as it filled with shadows and colors. A white tugboat passed, pulling a barge, heavy with its load. Its bow steered around a rowboat. Nigâr's admirer looked at the mansion's large roof for a while and then turned his head slowly to the young woman and asked:

"What is this entourage where desires burn like resplendent candles? Will you help me understand this, Nigâr?"

Nigâr laughed and said, "Aunt Ziba's entourage."

"Aunt Ziba's entourage is that lively and special?"

"Yes, Macid, it's very lively and quite special, though it is made up of the elements of life that everyone already knows: love, spite, envy, music, wine. Simple things like singing in the moonlight make up the very foundation of this world. And what a limitless love it is! What profound spite and envy! How much music, how much wine, how much singing, Macid! In this world, everything is pushed to its limit. The music continues until morning, wine is drunk to the last drop, and the *muhabbet* lasts a lifetime. When finished with this feast, a person is filled to the brim, replete and overflowing, having tasted all types of spiritual food from the sweetest to the most bitter."

"Like in the palace of an Oriental prince," Macid interjected.

Nigar continued, "A person supposes himself—though for an ephemeral time—to have power over everything like an Oriental prince, the ability to overturn, to crush, to break everything. He or she suddenly becomes all strength and ambition, prodigious from head to toe, and remains at that level of exhilaration."

Majid responded, "It's strange that a source of life this rich can be found in the entourage of a woman in her fifties...You almost resemble a young guru talking about the temple of a new god. There is zeal in your voice and fire in your eyes. There is definitely something different about you, Nigâr Abla!"

"This place is none other than a Bektashi lodge, Macid."

Macid looked into the face of his friend with a surprised gaze because, up until now, he knew her to be beyond every type of sectarian superstition.

It wasn't that he didn't know what a Bektashi lodge was. A few years before, when he had become interested in Islamic philosophy, an old and knowledgeable friend had given him quite a bit of information about Sufism and discussed the pillars and traditions of the Bektashi order with him. However, because Macid quickly gave up on his curiosity toward Islamic philosophy—which was the shortest lasting of his intellectual adventures—he did not benefit as much as he should have from the information of his scholarly friend; instead, he had contented himself with a few superficial and vague ideas about the Bektashi order and Sufism in general. To him, Sufism was a type of "mysticism" and

Bektashism was a primitive, roughly conceived form of "pantheism." As for the dervishes of this sect, Macid knew them as carefree, unrestrained, a bit skeptical and cynical. In his view, the Bektashi dervishes had departed from Islam and were nothing more than a few "Diogeneses" that had lost their purity.[1] For this reason, the young man could make no sense of a delicate and refined woman like his beloved Nigâr showing feelings resembling enthusiasm and excitement in the company of miscreants like these. As he thought about this, his amazement increased:

"A Bektashi lodge? What are you saying, Nigâr?"

Nigâr liked seeing the naïve astonishment of her young friend. Until now, she had always learned everything from him, though it was always theoretical, as if from a book. Now that the tables had turned, she felt a childish joy in possessing information to impart to him. In a voice trembling with excitement, she told him the story of this last week of adventure—after the night that she went to her aunt's house, being swept away in a strange current, she also went once as a visitor to the lodge. Gradually, she delved into details. She talked about Nasib and Rauf, Nur Baba and Ziba. She explained how they made love without a care. She told of the wine, the spread of *mezes*, the hymns, the singing in the moonlight, the master's glances, and his voice.

Macid found his young friend's words brimming with an unprecedented bit of eloquence. At one point, it seemed to him as if she were practically reading a page from Pierre Loti.[2] He listened with an artistic and sweet enthusiasm to quite a few parts of the story because, like all his colleagues, he was accustomed to seeing and loving the Orient, Oriental life, and Oriental scenes in the constructed ceremonies of Western literature and said repeatedly to himself: "Farrère should see this, Loti should hear this. What a different world this is!"[3] By the end of the story, the young woman talked only about Nur Baba's voice, and in that moment, the dark-haired young man's forehead scrunched up with painful anxiety because, like all secret admirers, he was overflowing and illogical in his jealousy.

"Nigâr," he said "Please help me see all this for myself just once. The truth is, I didn't know that there were nooks and crannies of our lives in this country so worthy of analysis and observation. This could be prime material

---

1 The Greek Cynic Diogenes of Sinope (d. ca. 320 BCE) is remembered as having led an ascetic lifestyle—for example, choosing to live in a tub in Athens rather than a house—and to have flaunted social conventions for which he was given the epithet "Diogenes the Dog." The Greek term *cynic* literally means "dog-like." The well-known story about Diogenes walking around with a lantern during the daytime in search of a true human being is popular in Sufi writings.

2 Pierre Loti was the penname of Louis-Marie-Julien Viaud (1850–1923) a French naval officer and author who wrote about Istanbul with romantic gusto and heavy doses of Orientalism. A café in Eyüp with a panoramic view of the Golden Horn is named after him.

3 Claude Farrère (1876–1957) was the penname of Frédéric-Charles-Pierre-Edouard Bargone, a French naval officer and novelist who set his novels in various Asian and Middle Eastern cities. Following World War I, he supported the Turkish national movement and visited Mustafa Kemal [Atatürk] at İzmit in 1922.

for a sociologist or even a sociological novel. It's such an exemplary specimen of oriental society."

Nigâr smiled lightly and said, "But there one can't remain only a spectator—somehow, unknowingly, unwillingly, one enters the game."

At this, the young man responded with a slightly angry voice, "This depends on the person. There are some people who, because they lack a strong or distinct personality, get lost in the atmosphere of any such group and lose themselves. But the others…" He paused, not feeling the need to complete his sentence. He instead said laughingly, "Ah, what the hell, let's try it one time, Nigâr Abla!"

The young woman, deep down, regarded this proposition of Macid's as impossible. Even the possibility of herself returning there again seemed to be a implausible and dangerous idea. After that bizarre night she spent at her aunt's and the following days, her visit to the lodge now seemed to her so strange and dreamlike that she felt as if she were living someone else's adventure. Nevertheless, Nigâr was not far enough away either in time or in distance from these two episodes to feel like this. It had been just three or four days since then, and in that time, not a day passed in which she did not come face to face with one of the people that reminded her of that experience. Nasib came to the waterfront mansion nearly every day, criticizing Madame Ziba constantly and talking about Nur Baba and Rauf, and at the same time clearly trying to pull Nigâr into her world. Even Celile had come to visit her two days before, bearing greetings from Nur Baba. Nigâr had received word yesterday that the lodge always desired her presence, even if she was only an outsider, a non-member.

In short, one could say that, for one week, the young woman was living uninterruptedly the drama and happenings of the lodge with her aunt Ziba, and this strange new world was, like an unseen spider, drawing her into its web quietly, every day bringing her a bit closer. But, despite all this, how was her heart confused with secrets responsible for the feeling that prevented her from seeing this world with fearless and familiar eyes? She herself could not distinguish this very well. She could only see that she had agonized for days, paralyzed by anxiety and fits of trembling, pulled in two directions by opposite forces.

Nigâr collected herself as if she were shaking off a deep sleep, and said to her young friend:

"Let's get up now, Macid. The air is damp and I think that they haven't taken the children inside."

6   An Unprecedented Ceremony in the Lodge of Nur Baba

Part I

Today, Dervish Çinari, the laborer and diligent cook of Nur Baba's lodge, had not taken a break since dawn, not even for two minutes. By himself, he sacrificed three sheep, carried on his back the equivalent of a cart full of grain from the gate all the way to the kitchen and placed the sacks one by one in the pantry, then moved over to the stove, cooked four pots of food, and prepared the *mezes* for the banquet, all of which he did with a cheerful enthusiasm until evening. It took a lion's strength to do this much work in one day. But the fundamental oddity was that Dervish Çinari showed no sign of fatigue and never complained. On the contrary, as the work increased, his enthusiasm and good cheer increased as well. He sang *nefes* hymns as he carried a load and, while working at the stove, sang a *gazel*.[1] Especially on days like this, when he was completely overwhelmed with work, the kitchen was filled with his singing.

Although there were certainly people in the lodge available to assist him, he would never accept help because he was very protective of his position. How many homeless aunties and female disciples had taken refuge in Nur Baba's lodge, drinking wine uninterrupted, from dawn to dusk and sleeping away their days because of unemployment or psychological troubles or having nothing better to do? Actually, most of them weren't in the lodge all the time, but on the days of the *Ayin-i Cem*—the Gathering Ceremony—they were present for certain, from morning onward. Dervish Çinari, who was generally shy around people and showed very little affection toward others, could not suffer the likes of these disciples at all. Because, for him, those who did not serve the lodge full-time did not count as true disciples and could only serve the lodge by giving money. To him, physical work performed by them would amount to nothing next to their financial support because he was a person who would call a gold coin "God" "if only it hadn't been round," like the dervish in a

---

1 Literally, *nefes* means "breath." In Bektashi parlance, a *nefes* is type of Bektashi hymn that usually takes the form of quatrains in the *hece* meter and holds an important place in ritual life and, as a form of literature, in expressing spiritual outlook and mystical experience. A *gazel* is a lyric poem of 4–15 couplets with a rhyming first couplet and all subsquent second hemstichs (half-lines of verse) rhyming with the hemstichs of the initial couplet.

DOI: 10.4324/9781003381471-7

famous Bektashi joke.[2] For him, gold was similar to God Almighty in two respects: first, it can't be held or seen with the eye, and second, its spell and power is evident in everything.[3]

Since the age of eighteen—that is, for almost forty-five years—Dervish Çinari has worn the large circular earring of blessing that is particular to the celibate dervishes.[4] Never in his life had he known the love of a father, or the tenderness of a son, not even the love of a woman. His entire youth passed by in a drunken and listless state. Nevertheless, he himself was of the opinion that he had seen and heard a great deal and, every now and then, he attempted to make others believe this as well. Perhaps Dervish Çinari had traveled to many places, perhaps he went as far as India and China with his master, Atif Baba. He had done a stint of service in many lodges, but not once in his life did he sober up enough to have appreciated his surroundings. The only time he was separated from his wine bottle was when he slept. Due to this powerful habit, Dervish Çinari had, for years, been in a state of sleepwalking from which he never awoke. All his actions seemed to emanate from the impulses of a never-ending dream. The only things he did clearly and correctly were the lodges' tasks of hard labor, each of which had become ingrained habits for him. It was for this reason that, on this particular day, he was feeling that he had lived in the fullest sense and could not find a way to end his exertions. Anyway, there was a mountain of work to be done, for there was an unprecedented ceremony in the lodge tonight. For tonight, Şerif Pasha's wife, the niece of Madame Ziba—Nigâr—was going to take initiation.[5]

This day, that Nur Baba had awaited for months in a state of intense worry, anxiety, and suffering, had begun in all its pomp and circumstance. The young Sufi master couldn't remember a day so important in his life. This evening, in his own lodge, he was not only preparing a celebration in the honor of a woman unique in both beauty and wealth, but also he was celebrating simultaneously the rare and outstanding success of his own power. In fact, this victory was in no way a product of his own power because it wasn't only *his* light that attracted Nigâr, a pale and timid moth, to the rambunctious

---

2 Unfortunately, we have been unable to locate this "famous" joke, so the context remains unclear. Tentatively, I would suggest that the joke is that the dervish respects money so much that he would revere it as a deity or *the* deity if only it didn't have a physical form, the idea of God having a shape or being circumscribed by form being unacceptable.

3 His first respect is humorous in the sense that it suggests that the dervish never sees or possesses a gold coin, and, if he does, he spends it.

4 This refers to the celibate class of dervishes known as *mücerred*. Being initiated into celibate dervishhood involves the ritual of piercing the ear, traditionally done at the threshold of Balım Evi at the central *dergâh* (shrine) in Hacı Bektaş. Different types of earrings can be worn, including the circular one mentioned here, as well as the heavy horse-shoe shaped *menguş*. The celibate branch traces its origins to the person of Balım Sultan: John Kingsley Birge, *The Bektashi Order of Dervishes* (London: Luzac, 1965), 164–165.

5 For unknown reasons, the author has used the name Şerif here instead of Eşref for Nigâr's husband. Eşref is used in all other cases in the novel. While this may be an error, I keep it to preserve the nature of the original text.

Figure 6.1 Bektashi Dervish with begging bowl (*keşkül*) (ca. 1895). "Derviche Bectachie," by Mihran Iranian. The dervish carries a begging bowl and wears a belt with a *teslim taşı* ("stone of surrender"), a distinctive Bektashi object whose twelve points represent the Twelve Imams.

Source: Courtesy of the *Suna ve İnan Kıraç Vakfı Fotoğraf Koleksiyonu / Suna ve İnan Kıraç* Foundation Photograph Collection, Catalog no: FKA 000617.

celebration of divine love on this night. No, the forces that attracted Nigâr here were legion, so many, that even the young woman herself was incapable of realizing or distinguishing the nature of the motives impelling her. She knew very well that one of the forces influencing her was Nasib. Since last summer, this woman hadn't ceased for one moment to encourage and lead Nigâr astray, like a joyful and mischievous devil. Recently, many of the disciples had come to her aid in this effort. So much so that the waterside house in Kanlıca practically turned into a second meeting place for these strange people and, one day, Nigâr realized that she had withdrawn from the company of her old friends, one by one. Since her nature was friendly and sociable, and her heart was as soft as her body, she found this invasion of her home and privacy impossible to resist and let herself be blown in any direction. Thank goodness that, together with Nigâr's mother, her admirer, the young Macid, was not a stranger to this moment in her life and watched over those present, all the while quietly envying Nigâr. They knew that his presence, if only for a while, was all that prevented them from gradually turning the house into a suffocating den of debauchery. Otherwise, within a year, Nigâr's salon would have been transformed into the halls and terraces of Madame Ziba's mansion in Çamlıca; it would have been overrun to that extent.

Without realizing it, Nigâr had been preparing for a day such as this for a year now. She had long since become accostumed to the smell of *rakı* and had begun to play *nefes* hymns on her piano. When responding to Nur Baba's greeting with the phrase, "I love and offer supplication, Master," she experienced the same distinctive pleasure experienced by someone who has learned a new language. Gradually, she found yet another enjoyment in imitating the gestures and etiquette required of the disciples by the code of the order—when giving thanks, they placed the right hand over the heart and bent forward. When entering a door, they passed through without stepping on the threshhold, and when they taught her the particularities of giving and receiving her *rakı* glass, she felt an almost childish joy.

However, it would be foolish to believe that Nigâr found the courage to leave behind her life solely under the influence of reckless impulses like these. She was essentially a serious but weak-willed woman, whose life was as drowsy as the silence of a newborn baby in a bright white cradle. It took more for her to submerge herself in this swirling, murky entourage that burned, in her own words, like a thousand desires, a thousand types of candles. No, Nigâr was not felled on Nur Baba's intricately woven red carpet with the submissiveness of a pigeon with its wings clipped. This particular pigeon fell on his carpet wounded in the heart by a stray bullet, a bullet that came from a dangerous weapon that Madame Ziba always shook back and forth in her hand, with a hopeless nervousness, in order to defend the happiness that had recently been exposed to numerous dangers. At the same time, it's true that this weapon had wounded her too. One by one, all of her attempts backfired. However much she wanted to drive Nigâr away from the lodge of Nur Baba, Nigâr came that much closer. Already, last summer, on the wide terrace of the mansion, when she told Nigâr, "You're not capable of being guided," Madame Ziba had unwittingly committed her first error and, with her own hands, had pushed the young woman into this fate. After this, everything she did only reinforced and repeated this first mistake. However, the miserable Madame Ziba had lost her senses so completely that she didn't understand what a dangerous thing it is to play with another woman's honor. Only after today's confirmation did she finally realize that even a bland, weak-willed woman like her young niece Nigâr could be equipped with the same fiery stubborness and jealousy that had writhed like a snake in her own breast for years. And she thought that, when this hitherto slumbering temper was irritated, Nigâr would respond with nothing but cold indifference. And repeating her folly, the first person who appeared before Nigâr to offer guidance was yet again Madame Ziba.

Since noon, Nur Baba had been sitting on the lodge's roof with binoculars, eyeing the road with childish anxiety. It wasn't until dusk that he finally saw Nigâr getting out of her aunt's long, pink-curtained carriage. Running to the top of the stairs in shock mixed with joy, he called out to Celile, who was pulling out a bed set for guests in the hall downstairs:

"Celile, Celile! Ziba's coming too. They're both coming together."

Nevertheless, as the carriage approached the door of the yard, it became clear that the arrivals were not just the two ladies but also one of Madame Ziba's servants and a tall young man. Nur Baba came down from the terrace, leaping four steps at a time. He had donned a fine pink robe, and emerged like the wind on the balcony of the hall, waving a hankerchief at the new arrivals with a playful bit of hospitality. However, when he saw the young man, his joy soured, and he said to Celile, who was hesitantly sticking her white head out the window:

"Oh, what hussies! Did you see that? They brought that boy with them!"

Celile, with a voice that concealed a touch of mockery, said slowly:

"What's their sin? Perhaps you didn't satisfy them, Your Sainthood?"

Nur Baba still continued to shake his hankerchief in an unwilling manner.

"What do I know? This must be some kind of joke." He continued, clenching his teeth. "This is all Ziba's doing…I'll make her pay for it!"

It was true that it was mostly Madame Ziba who had encouraged Macid to be Nigâr's *musahip*, her spiritual companion in the initiation. One day she had said half-serious, half-jokingly to Nur Baba:

"Nigâr will come. However, she has a lively shadow and will only come if he is allowed to accompany her. Will you agree to that?"

Unwittingly, Nur Baba agreed. And with that, Madame Ziba positioned him opposite a *fait accompli*. Nevertheless, this situation did not prevent Nur Baba from greeting Nigâr and Macid with extraordinary affection at the top of the stairs. He so effectively hid his selfish worries that even Macid, who was amazed and perplexed by the entire atmosphere, was made to feel at ease by the young shaykh's warm and sincere gestures.

7 An Unprecedented Ceremony in the Lodge of Nur Baba

Part II

Taken from Macid's diary:

...Aunt Ziba has finally pulled me into her strange world as well. Since last evening, I too am supposedly a Bektashi. In part, this came to pass due to my own interest, but it was mostly through vigorous encouragement from Aunt Ziba. Though she never said a word, Nigâr always opposed my participation in this ridiculous endeavor. I don't know why.

The truth is that her attitude also increased my interest and curiosity. Otherwise, the Bektashi order would have remained a secret to me as well. Though at this moment I find neither great detriment nor great benefit whether it remains a secret or not, yesterday I felt differently. I spent the entire day anxious and worried in a way that I hadn't been for some time. As Aunt Ziba's carriage took us to the place said to be the lodge, I was so preoccupied and immersed in thought that I was barely aware of my surroundings or of Nigâr's dear face. Now and then, I asked Aunt Ziba, "I beg you. Please tell me. What am I going to see? What am I going to do? What am I going to become?" I knew that I would be required to perform a number of movements I was unaccustomed to, like kneeling, kissing the ground, and bowing for hours in front of a shaykh. Deep down, I had already resolved to comply with all this. Nevertheless, I nearly turned back from my decision as I considered the possibility that the Bektashi protocol would entail more pointless, ridiculous, degrading, and taxing obligations than the pious gestures and physical movements performed by adherents of all Eastern religions. Moreover, seeing Nigâr in front of me, refined and perfumed wearing clean, elegant, and refined attire, my heart filled with a different dread, for her sake. I asked her several times, "Are you sure that what we're doing is rational?" She looked at my face as if she didn't understand. For how long had she accustomed herself to this lethargic state? Her once-brilliant eyes had lost their old luster. A disturbing, enigmatic cloud covered the transparent face that, just a few months earlier, had been a spotless mirror reflecting her pure soul to me. Since that time, I haven't been able to make any sense of her behavior. For instance, what is the reason behind this unthinkable escapade? Bektashism and Nigâr are worlds apart. Isn't all of this contrary to her education, to her mind, to the knowledge she has obtained, to her way of living, thinking, and dressing? I wonder,

DOI: 10.4324/9781003381471-8

has she too become prey to that young dervish who has been squeezing her aunt in his claw for years? I don't find this likely either. For five years, my sole occupation has been to read and to memorize every aspect of this woman, so I know that Nigâr is a tranquil woman who enjoys her comfort. She knows that she is beautiful and likes to be loved. However, loving others is never her business. The only one she can love is herself. How many times have I seen her gazing admiringly at her own figure in front of a large mirror?

As soon as Madame Ziba's voice gave us the news "We're here," I shook as if arousing from sleep. The carriage stopped in front of the wooden gate of a ruined and secluded property with crumbling walls. Inside, it was half-vegetable garden, half-orchard, and there was a section with a graveyard as well. A large piece of stone hung on the door, either to support it or to use as a knocker.

Madame Ziba's elegant, white-gloved hand pushed open this coarse, strange door. Slowly, we began to ascend the dim, unkempt path that formed a rather long, steep climb, with Ziba in front, Nigâr and I side by side, and the servant named Peykar in the rear. From afar, parts of a large, unpainted, old wooden mansion appeared between the trees, and, on the top floor of this mansion, from a balcony that rested on wooden supports, a man dressed in pink was waving a handkerchief at us. Both Nigâr and Aunt Ziba reciprocated. I detest these kinds of niceties. It's not my style to convey my feelings with this type of gesture when departing or arriving. Previously, Nigâr didn't care for affectations like this either, but now she seems quite accustomed to it all, especially to this place we have entered. She knows everyone here quite well. For instance, while we were walking, she practically exchanged jokes with a half-crazy, bizarre dervish with pierced ears and his sleeves rolled-up, who had jumped in front of us from some corner of the yard as a surprise. A little later, Nigâr exchanged greetings in a manner particular to the Bektashis with a host of women large and small, young and old. Then, with the tenderness of a mother and daughter, she kissed and hugged a white-haired, but kohl-eyed, woman at the top of the stairs—this was the shaykh's wife. As for me standing a bit behind her, I was in a dizzy, awful state that disoriented my words, looks, steps, and movements. I felt as if I had fallen by chance among the creatures of another world. If nothing else, Nigâr should have felt that she was associating with persons far below her because, at first sight, none of the faces that I could see in my state of bewilderment, not one, inspired any trust, let alone friendship. However, despite the pink robe, the cone-shaped hat, and the disheveled hair, I found the shaykh greeting us at the top of the stairs to be quite charming. This young shaykh had warm, sensitive eyes that appeared to understand everything. He greeted me with sincerity and warmth, said that he had heard much about me, and took me into a spacious room. The women went into another chamber to take off their coats.

The room we entered was bare, furnished in white, and full of evening sun-light; a different view opened out from each of the open windows. There was nothing more to fill the eye than two seating cushions facing each other and a few straw chairs. Only the shaykh's personal corner above the cushion of honor was a bit more ornate. It was furnished with large and small silken pillows and three layers of thin, fringed mattresses. Beside this was another space, belonging to his wife. Such arbitrary and self-worshipping class organization of the lodge leaders seemed very strange to me, but what really struck me as bizarre were the calligraphic panels and drawings on the walls. These pictures must have been drawn by a child and painted by a lunatic: one showed a dervish sitting cross-legged on top of the earth, smoking a pipe; another, an ascetic immersed in meditation on top of a number of human-eyed, thrashing birds, eight-legged tigers, and a four-headed dragon; another portion of these pictures, depicting Ali's raids, appear to have come from an extremely rudimentary and unskilled hand.[1] Among these pictures, there were also a great number of calligraphic panels with intricate calligraphic lines and simple meanings—for instance, there were a number of large and small panels with "*Ya Ali*" ("Oh Ali") written on them, and a large frame, hanging above the door of the room, contained this couplet:[2]

> *Mejnun left me to the abode of time*
> *From mad wanderer to mad wanderer, it remains a house of ruins*

I imagine that Bektashis look at life through this lens. Seeing my gaze focused on the walls, the shaykh began to give explanations of each of the pictures. I asked him, in particular, about the symbols comprised by the ascetic in the middle of that host of strange creatures. According to him, this was simply "Kaygusuz Sultan's" picture.[3] The shaykh also showed me the depictions of Ali's mule, "Düldül," and "Zülfikar," his two-pointed sword. He appeared to give some importance to all these trifles, and I imagine that he was then striving to guide me via these lines and colors to the symbols and secrets of the Sufi path, which I would soon enter. This man was not nearly as mature and profound as he seemed as first. His words were quite simplistic and childish. However, he did not cease to be charming for a moment. Though some of his gestures were overly friendly, he didn't make

---

1 This refers to Ali (b. ca. 600, d. 661 CE), the cousin and son-in-law of the Prophet Muhammad. For the Shi'a and the Bektashis, he is the first Imam—a figure of immense cosmic and spiritual importance, while for the Sunnis, he is understood as the fourth caliph, the last of the "rightly guided" caliphs.
2 Such calligraphic panels are common in Bektashi and other Sufi lodges.
3 Kaygusuz Abdal, whose name means "care-free dervish," here referred to as "Sultan," was a poet, author, and mystic, who left behind a rich collection of poetry, sermons, and epistles written in Anatolian Turkish. He was one of the first poets to call himself "Bektashi" and, as such, is considered to be a founder of Alevi-Bektaşi literature. A depiction of him was present in almost every Bektashi lodge. While information about his life is difficult to verify, he is remembered as founding a Bektashi lodge near Cairo and traveling widely throughout the Eastern Mediterranean. One hagiography places his death at 848/1444: Ahmet T. Karamustafa, "Kaygusuz Abdal: A Medieval Turkish Saint and the Formation of Vernacular Islam in Anatolia," in *Unity in Diversity*, ed. Orkhan Mir-Kasimov (Leiden & Boston, MA: Brill, 2014), 329–342.

Figure 7.1 Calligraphic Panel: "Bektashi invocation to Ali" ("Ya Ali"), Anonymous. The name "Ali" is written with the ع (*ayn*) character as a face composed of two "ʿAli"s and the letter ى (*ya*) as the sword Zülfikar. The Bektashi head-gear (*tac*) is composed of letters spelling: *ya Hazret Hacı Bektaş Veli* (O, Saint Haji Bektash).
Source: Courtesy of the Collection of İrvin Cemil Schick.

a bad impression. After finishing the explanation of the calligraphic panels, he slowly sat down in his place and assumed a position that was something between squatting and sitting cross-legged on top of three layers of thin mattresses.

Then the women joined us. Aunt Ziba was more ornate than ever; her eye-liner and dyed hair virtually dazzled. Her outfit was as flamboyant and gaudy as a *prima donna* in an opera. In comparison with her, Nigâr was quite plain, but she had dressed with care. Her dark red blouse with the collar half open gave her skin an elegant fairness. On her neck lay a necklace made of a line of coral and a few black pearls. This would be one of the gifts that her husband had sent to her from Spain. How surprised Eşref Pasha would be if he saw her here! As the room filled with the women I had seen earlier, I understood with greater clarity just how far Nigâr had fallen from her own social circle. Though these women respected the preservation of the distance between themselves and women like Aunt Ziba or Nigâr and wandered in the rooms and halls of the lodge with the demeanor of servants or spoiled parasites, it did not prevent them, however, from sitting beside Nigâr or whispering something in her ear and chuckling or making excessive demonstrations of friendship, like hugging Aunt Ziba and saying, "Oh remember the good old days, you pistol!" Among them was an old woman called Lady Alhotoz Afife. On the tangled lines of her face, one could read a life story that was turbid from start to finish. However, after the shaykh's wife, she was treated as the most privileged person of the lodge. The penetrating, harsh expression of her eyes made one's soul shudder, and her speech was full of crass jokes. This woman walked around the room for a while, made a gesture to Aunt Ziba, a joke to the shaykh, an innuendo to the shaykh's wife, and then she fixed her eyes on Nigâr, came over, and squeezed between her and me. She reeked of alcohol, like the handkerchief of a drunkard.

I guessed that Nigâr already knew the woman because she didn't seem surprised at all when she deliberately sat between us or by her excessively affectionate behavior. She even performed the courtesy of twice extending her fresh cheek to that woman's disfigured mouth. The shaykh's wife examined me from the opposite cushion. A few times, our gazes met. The truth is that out of all the murky faces, only this woman gave me a feeling of cleanliness, order, and chastity, due to her clothing and her mannerisms. Her white hair lent nobility to her face. Once in a while, she rose in a commanding manner and whispered orders to those wandering in the hall.

All of a sudden, laughing heartily, the shaykh sitting in the corner announced:

"Ha, our community is coming."

After this, we all got up and looked out the window. From among the trees, a horde of men came toward us—one with a bottle in hand, another with a drum, another with an *oud*.

Aunt Ziba asked, "Where did this group come from?"

Continuing to laugh, the shaykh replied, "From under two pine trees. They began *muhabbet* in the morning."

"*Muhabbet*" in Bektashi terminology would mean to drink, to play instruments, etc. And, indeed, the ones arriving seemed to have drunk quite a lot. Some among them had shouldered their jackets and taken their ties in hand, laughing loudly and joking with one another. A little behind them walked a man who was either too drunk or partially disabled, leaning on a dervish, who had a long, snowy beard.

A little later, they filled the room where we sat and the shaykh introduced each of them to me. I say "me," because Nigâr already knew them. The only one she didn't know was the snowy-bearded shaykh, so he felt obliged to introduce himself to her: "Latif Baba, your guide."

Like all the other gentlemen, our guide Latif Baba was quite uninhibited. He wore a short jacket with no sleeves, a belt with a large, matte-stone buckle, and from the buttonhole of his outer shirt hung a line of red, green, and white crystal pieces on short, thin chains. Turning his bulky body toward Nigâr and me, he asked in the old Balkan dialect:

"Master, are these the new souls?"

All these faces, these words, these voices, these people, and the air of this room were gradually depressing me even more, and I almost lost it when I saw Nigâr breathing comfortably right beside me. She responded with that ever-present white smile that pulls just so to the side of her mouth, giving her face the most exquisite expression. She looked at everyone with a flattering gaze. How had I failed to understand her for so many years?

A few times she looked out the window and said:

"Where is Nasib? Is she not coming, I wonder?"

This Lady Nasib is the woman that dragged Nigâr to this dump. How many times have I run into her at the waterfront mansion? How many times have I stumbled upon her and Nigâr huddled together, talking secretively? No matter where she is, she will come to watch this spectacle of her own making. As a matter of fact, a short spell later, the shaykh, who kept his eye on the yard, turned to Nigâr with a flirtatious smile and said:

"Don't worry, wherever she is, she will turn up because Sir Rauf is visiting."

Together, everyone imitated the shaykh's laugh. Nigâr restrained herself, preserving her ever-present smile and looked ahead blushing a bit. This Sir Rauf was one of the young men with a rosewood cane with a silver shaft, a satin-collared overcoat, and a thin curled mustache. That is, he was a civil servant of the new generation.[4] Judging by the statement of the shaykh that caused so many complicit smiles, he was clearly the lover of Nasib. After the young man entered the room, kissed the shaykh's knees according to protocol, and sat in his place, he answered those asking about Nasib in a deliberately suggestive manner...

Poor Nasib. She only managed to arrive at dusk as the lamps began to glow. Dressed in lace and covered in perfume, her rotund body overflowed with excitement. In order to come here, what obstacles she had encountered, what dangers! Had she not driven off the visitors that dropped by unexpectedly that night, had she not told a host of lies to her husband whom she saw on the way, had she not been obliged to leave her child who had been burning with a 39C° fever for two days with a new nanny, and, finally, had her carriage not come face to face with her father's at the bend in the road leading to the lodge? As Nasib explained all this, her gaze turned to Rauf from time to time. For whatever reason, Aunt Ziba listened to the young woman's words with a rude and contemptuous smile. Nigâr was shocked by the story. Among those in the room was a man by the name of Sir Necati, who said:

---

4 Here the author refers to the men associated with the new bureaucratic institutions that emerged during the Tanzimat era (1839–56), who developed a new sartorial style that blended European fashion with the fez. The coat known as the 'İstanbulin' is associated with this new bureaucratic cohort. In the novel *Kiralık Konak* (1921), Yakup Kadri Karaosmanoğlu wrote about this garment with high praise: "In Istanbul, there were two eras, first that of the Istanbulin and the other that of the frock coat…At no other time did the Ottomans attain the same level of elegance, cleanliness, and refinement as that of the İstanbulin period. The greatest product of the Auspicious Tanzimat was the Istanbulite gentleman in an İstanbulin."

"Running into your father is the unfortunate thing, Madame, not running into your husband."

Everyone began to laugh. I'm gradually coming to better understand the meaning of Bektashi lodges: they are most certainly institutions established in opposition to family life.

The wife of the shaykh who had gone outside with our guide, that snowy-bearded dervish, approached us with a large towel whose edges were ornately embroidered; he bent over, first to Nigâr and then to me, and said:

"Come, Sir, it's time. Do your ablutions in the water, your guide is waiting."

Then turning to the shaykh, she said, "Master, everything is ready. Shall we begin?"

This Bektashi ablution is something completely unusual. Though the water makes less contact on the designated parts of the body than the ablutions taken five times a day, they believe that it lasts for the rest of your life. I don't know to what degree this is true, because our guide gave us this information in a half-joking, half-serious manner. First, Nigâr performed her ablutions. The guide simultaneously poured water on her with a pitcher and taught her the prayer that needed to be recited. This prayer was quite simple and was recited in Turkish. For example, as the ears got wet:

"From now on these ears will be closed against curses and gossip."

As the eyes became wet:

"These eyes will be as if they had not seen what they saw."

Coming to the feet, "These feet will not deviate from God's path," and so on.

Nigâr spoke all of these with a trembling voice, attentiveness, and importance, as if she were doing something deadly serious. By the end of the ablution, particularly when her feet were being washed, she had goosebumps from head to toe. I went through my washing more or less enraged and almost grumbling aloud. My inner voice said, "What's happening to me? Damn you all."

If I had only known what else was in store for me. After finishing the ablution ceremony, we were taken to the door of the meeting hall, in their expression, "bare foot and bald headed." This place they call the *"meydan"* was a wide rectangular space in the lower floor of the lodge, enclosed in glass in the style of a mosque. The walls were covered from top to bottom with hangings of the order and the floor was checkered with white, black, and red carpets.[5]

The *meydan*'s north side was the "place of guidance," which formed the prayer niche for the disciples. Before sitting down, all those who entered kissed the side of a piece of white marble shaped like a funeral slab. They did so with many ritual acts of reverence and worship. On each corner of this stone, a

---

5 On the image in Figure 7.2, important in Bektashi visual art, see: İrvin Cemil Schick, "Hz. Ali ve Devesi Levhaları" in *Deve Kitabı* eds. Erkan Demir and Emine Gürsoy Naskali (Istanbul: Kitabevi Yayınları, 2014), 5–40.

Figure 7.2 Calligraphic Panel: "Ali driving the camel with his own coffin," Anonymous. This exquisite piece depicts a widespread Bektashi story in which Hasan and Husayn are carrying Ali's coffin to the burial site and request that the camel driver lift his veil. When he does so, they realize that the driver is also Ali.

Source: Courtesy of the Collection of İrvin Cemil Schick.

thick, meter-long candle was burning and, on top, stood a silver candleholder with forty arms holding unlit candles. The master sat beside this stone, still as a dead man with his eyes closed, his hands stuck in the sleeves of his cloak, squatting on top of his own rug, wearing a black turban and a folded conical hat on his head and a wide white cloak on his back. In this attire, he resembled an icon of an Asian god. His wife entered first. She walked toward the white stone with her hands clasped on her chest, crossing each other. As she moved across the *meydan*, she stopped every three steps and prostrated herself. When she reached the stone, she bowed and kissed it, and then walked to the shaykh making the same movements, in the shape of semi-circle in the *meydan*, and bowed at his knees, and then, showing the same reverence to her own carpet, finally sat down. Following her, lines of men entered. At first glance, I thought that if nothing else, this order outwardly gave women equal rights. However, in its ritual, the women formed the back row, and rights of priority, like age and seniority, were of secondary importance to the privilege given by manhood. Therefore, I too entered the *meydan* before Nigâr. More accurately, our guide entered before both of us. Despite some physical misfortunes, like obesity and inebriation, this man followed several extra rituals that were more difficult than what the others had performed. For instance, while entering, he kissed the threshold of the door. Then on every third step while walking, he recited some ritualistic phrases—sometimes in Arabic, sometimes in Persian, sometimes in clear Turkish. He waited for the shaykh's responses before advancing. Then, with a flame taken from a long, thick candle, he lit, one by one, the forty candles in the candleholder with forty arms.[6] During this task, his lips did not desist from murmuring a number of prayers without interruption. Quite a few times, he prostrated in front of the shaykh, got up, prostrated again, and, then, moving backward while keeping his face toward the shaykh, went outside. Nigâr and I were waiting for him in the half-darkness of the courtyard. In the *meydan*, there was a group of at least fifty men and women waiting, kneeling on the rugs that were all around in rows. Our guide came to me with a thin white thread in his hand and slowly tied it to my waist. He passed one part of it down my neck, wrapped one end of it around my thumb, and then took the other end in his own hand. Tied to one another, we tottered toward the threshold of the door. My guide stopped in front of the threshold and yelled with a deep voice:

"*Ya mufettihü'l-ebvab, Oh, Opener of Doors!*"[7]

The shaykh replied from inside the meydan in the same deep tone:

"We have opened a resplendent door for you!"

At these words, we both bowed at once and kissed the threshold. My guide spoke softly in my ear:

"Pass over without stepping on it."

I didn't understand. "What should I pass over without stepping on?"

The man pulling me by the neck with a string said:

"The threshold, my son, the threshold."

We passed the threshold without treading on it. After walking one or two steps inside, we turned our faces toward the master, who was surrounded by burning candles, and we prostrated on the floor again. Our standing up and walking became more difficult after kissing the threshold, jumping, and prostrating on the floor. What a secret skill there is in walking and stopping every three steps! During this moment of pause, which doesn't even last for a second, the big toe of the right foot quickly touches the big toe of the left foot, the torso bows slightly forward, the hand is pressed against the chest, and the eyes remain fixed only on the shaykh for one moment, and this is done so quickly and so repetitively that when a person is doing it, one almost

---

6 The candleholder with forty branches is known as the *Kırk Budak* (lit. "Forty Branches"), typically only used on important holidays like *Nevruz* and the Tenth of *Muharrem*. For Bektashis, the number 40 represents the forty saints or "Kırklar," who were inducted by Ali into the spiritual hierarchy at the house of Fatima (Tr. Fatma), Ali's wife and Muhammad's daughter. The *Kırklar* hold an important place in Bektashi belief, practice, and poetry.

7 The phrase is in Arabic in the original text with no translation provided. Here it is transliterated in the Turkish style so as to approximate the pronunciation by Turkish speaker.

loses control of the hands, the arms, the face, and especially the feet. By all appearances, one enters a kind of epileptic fit.

We stopped abruptly five steps from the shaykh. My guide started again with those mixed recitations in a loud voice. These recitations were laced with the names of many saints and prophets, almost like a page from a sacred history. Only toward the end did his words come to the actual ceremony. He uttered a few sentences that meant roughly:

"A soul whose eye does not see, whose ear does not hear, born again from his mother, a sacrificial lamb whose neck is tied, came to the house. He wishes to burn in the hearth of Haji Bektash. His eye wants to see. Will you accept what I have brought? I pose the question."

This sacrificial lamb was me. The master recited the guide's final words to the assembly word for word, demanding them to repeat after him and then added:

"Are you sure of the honesty and sincerity of this soul's hand and tongue?"

All together, they responded: "*Eyvallah*, Master!" Enthusiastic voices proclaiming "*Allahu Akbar—God is the greatest*" followed this. I heard women behind me crying. I bent my neck down in submission like a creature going to be slaughtered.

Pulling me by the neck, my shepherd slowly brought me in front of the shaykh. I squatted and bowed my head toward him. The Bektashis call this "submitting your head." Following instructions, I grasped the edge of the shaykh's robe with my right hand and let my left hand rest upon his with our thumbs bound together. The black-bearded shaykh brought his mouth close to my ear with the concerned sincerity of someone who is about to tell an important secret. Inside, I told myself, "Now I'm going to receive the Bektashi secret!" And for the first time since I entered the lodge, I was shaking with childish curiosity. Before long, I felt that my curiosity had been in vain. When I got up from the master's presence after this secret communication that lasted all of five minutes, there was only a thick cone-shaped hat on my head. Other than this, my head felt nothing profound or weighty. In my ears, I carried no wisdom but rather one or two vague sentences that made up the first and last of the shaykh's utterances:

"Will you control your hands, your loins, and your tongue and use them only for good purposes? If you're not going to be faithful, don't enter this path! Once you've chosen this path, don't turn back! The one who comes pays with his wealth, the one who turns back pays with his soul."

So, in my view, maybe perhaps the secret is nothing more than this. Following this, it was time, in the company of my guide, to kiss a number of unoccupied rugs whose owners were invisible. First that white stone of Balım Sultan is kissed, then the rug of Saint Haji Bektash, then the rug of Khorasan, after that Aşçı Baba's rug and finally, well, finally, I suppose that the new Bektashi collapses in a dizzy, exhausted state on the rug that is designated for him. How badly all these rugs smelled, these holy rugs which are kissed and prostrated upon! As if they were freshly skinned from the back of a goat...

What disgusting, senseless acts I have performed tonight! Without a doubt, acknowledging this episode of my life will be difficult for me. The contempt that I felt at the end of this strange ritual will always, *always* trouble me, like the penalty of a self-inflicted sin. What *was* I just a while before, among that fifty-person circle of spectators? In what position was I? Undoubtedly, I was as amusing as a clown unwittingly performing somersaults in a circus. As Nigâr's turn came, this suspicion in me was confirmed. She was also tied at the neck with a thin string to the big, snowy-bearded man in the middle of the *meydan*, sometimes pacing, sometimes prostrating on the floor. Her feet were bare and her hair was disheveled. Seeing her move, I felt my head bobbing involuntarily and my face turning bright red. This situation was not suitable for young, beautiful women: there is an endless calamity in their being amusing.

When she too had completed her torture, she squatted beside me. Following this, there were long prayers and acts of worship; rituals were performed in front of a door above which was written in Arabic, "*Wa aṭ'amūhum faqīran wa yatīman*" (*Feed them, the poor and the orphans*). Then the guide, who had been walking around continually, passed a large pitcher from hand to hand, beginning with the master and reciting the prayer "*wa saqāhum*" (*Give them to drink*), and people drank a red liquid from it. I have no information about the taste of the spirit because the pitcher had touched a total of fifty-five mouths by the time it reached me and among these was the black-toothed, disfigured grin of Alhotoz Afife. Apparently, the camaraderie of the Bektashis is established by these types of rituals. Actually, the fact that Nigâr, whom I knew to be so immaculate, did not refrain from showing enthusiasm while complying with this disgusting obligation, without protesting, sufficiently proved to me just how appropriate and effective these rituals are.

The Bektashi ceremony did not stop here. In fact, it had really just begun. In no time at all, the *meydan* transformed into a bizarre drinking house. The same people who knelt on rugs with complete reverence a bit earlier clustered around circular spreads of food and drink on the floor called *sofra*s, laughing, joking, and singing.[8] The *sofra*s appeared to be the cradles of drunken and festive nights. One can guess beforehand, with perfect clarity, in what condition those sitting around them will arise a bit later. Aside from the bulbous oversized decanters of *rakı* with ice, seeing the *mezes* alone brings sufficient understanding of how extravagant this feast will be. Good heavens! What did they *not* have in terms of food and drink on these *sofra*s? Without a doubt, the renowned feasts of Chinese princes were neither more sumptuous, nor more bountiful than these. I approached Nigâr and asked:

---

8 On the *sofra* and ritual meal, see: Soileau, "Spreading the Sofra."

"What army will consume all these plates and all these bottles?"

With the manner of a Kalendar,[9] which I was seeing in her for the first time, Nigâr said:

"Our stomachs."

"Maybe yours," I said, "but I'm so exhausted that I'm good for nothing except waiting for the morning by myself in a lonely place with longing and regret."

Nigâr found my anger irrational and misplaced. She shrugged her shoulders dismissively and said only, "You child!"

I was gradually beginning to hate her. She was convinced that she had walked toward a vast new horizon in life and had left me so far behind. It was as if she were delighted and filled with pride. She imitated her aunt in everything, and, like every imitator, she carried this parasitic identity with all its shortcomings and imperfections.

Just as when we sat down at the *sofra* (yes, despite everything I finally sat down), Nur Baba took Aunt Ziba on his right and Nigâr on his left. I squeezed between Aunt Ziba and someone named Necati. Later, other gentlemen— *beys*—and ladies—*hanıms*—took their places. Again, Alhotoz Afife did not leave Nigâr's side. Nasib and Rauf sat together intimately across from me. All together, we were fifteen women and men, and we formed the most important and privileged of the four *sofra*s that covered the *meydan*. At the others sat the dervishes that made up the second and third levels of the lodge in terms of position and respect. Nur Baba's wife simultaneously directed all the *sofra*s that sat adjacent to one another. In fact, this class organization was not compatible with the customs of dervishhood at all. I wonder in what respects these men, who call one another "brother," actually behave in a spirit of brotherhood and equality. It is certainly appropriate to hang calligraphic panels on the doors of Bektashi lodges with slogans like the Arabic phrase: "*Ikramū n-nās ʿalā qadar darajātihim*" (*Respect people according to their rank.*) Considering this, I noticed that even our *sofra* was divided into classes. For example, the master had a pink-colored *rakı* set, and there were *meze*s put on plates of this same color that only Aunt Ziba and Nigâr had been granted permission to eat from. We, the less fortunate, were drinking in turns from the single white glass and from the hand of an elderly woman wearing make-up by the name of Nuriye, who sat at the farthest corner of the *sofra*. Yes, you heard correctly: from a single shared glass! Despite everything, I let myself go with the flow. I wanted to get drunk quickly and fall asleep in an intoxicated stupor. It has happened a few times in my life that I have felt

---

9 The Kalendars were mainly wandering dervishes who renounced normal life and often flaunted social conventions. They are remembered for libertinism, a mendicant lifestyle, and their unconventional appearance which, in the Ottoman context, included piercings, wearing only animal skins, and shaving the head and eyebrows. See Ahmet Karamustafa, *Unruly Friends: Dervish Groups in the Islamic Later Middle Period, 1200–1550* (Oxford: Oneworld, 2006).

this strange need. Sometimes I delight in despising and humiliating myself via inebriation.

However, I had never seen Nigâr drink before. I was shocked seeing her presenting to her lips the pink glass that the young shaykh with the white robe and the languid gaze beside her handed to her now and then, while gently raising the edge of her mouth upward, smiling. Nigâr seemed to be quite accustomed to the ceremony with the glass; each time, she bowed with a number of courtesies and never forgot to kiss the cupbearer's hand, then bringing the empty cup to her chest with reverence. I don't know if it was because her cupbearer was the guide—she did this with even more zeal and respect than the others, adding much vivacity with her personality and elegance, such that all eyes at the *sofra* turned toward her involuntarily. People from other *sofra*s even began to come over to ours once in a while to catch a glimpse of her. Indeed, Nigâr's graces and charms were filling the group with intense curiosity, even causing shudders now and then. She was the object of everyone's gaze, first and foremost that of the shaykh. She seemed to have entered the lodge in a state of a instant brilliance. The eyes of everyone in the lodge seemed dazzled by her. Unquestionably, Nigâr was the youngest, the most beautiful, and the most exceptional of the women I saw that evening. Neither Aunt Ziba's power and pomp nor Nasib's brilliant and vivacious presence, nor the freshness of the two doe-eyed young girls said to be the nieces of Mother Celile, compared to one of her glances, one of her smiles, or to any of her perceptible and intangible qualities. Her smallest movements resembled music that bound together the spirit of all the people in a harmonious composition.

Maybe it is also the strength and importance of her purse that gave her this unique status. Beauty and wealth are the two great forces to which every head bows down in the Bektashi lodges. Nigâr combined both these forces in herself. Who knows how much this night of victory cost her. As for me, I remember spending more than ten *lira* for this strange entertainment, including the money placed beneath the shaykh's cushion this morning. Who knows how much poor Aunt Ziba had forked over here for the last ten years, she, who despite sitting now on the right side of the shaykh, looked in every respect like a dethroned queen? Actually, her position in the lodge was not yet lower than Nigâr's. Everyone still addressed her "Madame!" with worshipful yet excessive familiarity. For instance, five or six people would go running for the ashtray she had forgotten in her room or three or four would immediately bend down in front of her, vying to pick up her handkerchief that had fallen to the floor. But despite all this, on her face was the orphan-like depression of those who suffer in longing for another time and for a past prosperity. It seemed that the guide also felt this and he lavished attention on her. Sometimes he whispered things in her ear secretively; sometimes—I suppose the meaning was only known between the two of them—he tried to make her laugh and, once in a while, placed something from the *mezes* into her mouth with his own hand.

Nasib made the same gesture to Rauf, and Lady Alhotoz Afife to Nigâr. Nigâr appeared to be bored because of the old woman's troublesome and cold conversation and maybe also in part because the young master was neglecting her. With a few gestures, she indicated a need to sit beside me. However, I was busy trying to appear as if I were listening to Necati, the man sitting beside me since the beginning of the—however misplaced it is, let us use their expression—*muhabbet*. This Mr. Necati was a man saturated with the literature of Tavukpazarı:[10] he read poetic verses to me with the voice of a Kalendar, related his memories, and explained that a poet named Andelib drank I don't know how many liters of *rakı* in one day.[11] He himself was one of the powerful bureaucrats in the Ministry of Justice. Our *sofra* was made up of important and distinguished individuals like him, with the exception of Niyazi and our guide. Likewise, a bit farther down, there was one named Mr. Nesimi who was said to be the undersecretary of the Ministry of Pious Foundations;[12] opposite him sat a huge colonel wearing an open-breasted robe who had an enormous bald head that swung back in forth in both directions. More than a soldier, or, more accurately, more than a person, this man looked like a satyr from Greek mythology chasing after newly matured virgins. He was so occupied with the young girls beside him that he was oblivious to his surroundings. With suspicious, concealed gestures, he moved continuously, his cheeks full of *meze*s and his eyes gleaming. The only time this man collected himself a bit was when he sang a hymn, getting up on his knees to join in with his gruff voice.

The melodic and heavenly musical sessions of *muhabbet* didn't merely change this man's appearance, they gave the entire assembly a different vitality, bestowing a charming warmth. I honestly think that only the uniquely beautiful and meaningful thing in Bektashism is the collective singing of the hymns they call *nefes*. It is a strange orchestra comprised of women's and men's voices that channels a distinct fever of the disease called nostalgia with every blast of breath. The verses resemble the delirious mutterings of a senile spirituality that has passed through a number of intellectual and emotional episodes and crises, from a number of different geographical regions. With all its sorrow, intoxication, with all that awful sluggishness, it is the most distinctive Turkish music that exists. While I listened, they passed before my eyes, one by one: the pagan Turk riding bareback on mares with stiff manes;

10 Tavukpazarı is a neighborhood in the Fatih neighborhood of Istanbul, near the Grand Bazaar, that became famous as a site for drinking intoxicating beverages and reciting romantic poetry during the reign of Sultan Abdülhamid II (r. 1876–1909). It hosted many coffee houses and taverns where people could escape their woes and the oppressive political climate.

11 "Andelib" was the *nom de plume* of Mehmet Faik Esat (1290–1320/1873–1902). A journalist by profession, he worked as the chief editor of several different publications in Istanbul; more famously, his capacity for imbibing prodigious amounts of alcohol and composing verse were the stuff of legend.

12 The Ministry of Pious Foundations was the bureaucratic institution of state (founded in 1840) that managed property placed in the status of charitable foundations under the instrument of Islamic law named "*vakıf*" (Arabic: *waqf*).

the raider Turk twirling his lance at the edge of the walls of the cities whose splendor is the stuff of legends; the Muslim Turk listening to the life story of Muhammad in a Arab tent and hearing of the atrocity of Karbala in a Persian palace; and finally the urbane, debauched Turk immersed in mirth and dance around the overturned banquets of Caesars. I, and all those beside me, were the mixed product of these varied adventures. Nur Baba's face, in all its nuances, channeled the hedonist Turk. As for me, I represented with all the fever of my soul, the sentimental Turk. I don't know why, but Nigâr almost looked like the favorite woman of a prince. As for Aunt Ziba, there was no difference between her and the ostentatious madams of old that strolled around in three-layered robes through the sheltered audience halls and had long-haired servants rub their knees on the wide, eastern-style sofas. It was as if a veil fell from the faces of all those sitting around: what a specimen of an Eastern prostitute Nasib was! What a distinctive Istanbulite womanizer was Rauf! How much did Celile's two nieces remind one of two young dancing girls who had just taken the cymbals off their fingers! Colonel Hamdi had the mug of an undistinguished Janissary! How beautifully did Alhotoz Afife embody the old hag of our fables!

Toward midnight, a wildly festive mood took over the *meydan*. The master rose to dance the *sema* and several of the women joined him as well. Beginning with Alhotoz Afife, some mature women like her, this one and that, got down on their knees and began to sing passionate poems called *mani*s. There were people going to-and-fro between our *sofra* and theirs, and vice versa. Most of them were women around the age of forty-five who had plucked their faces of even the smallest hairs, or, conversely, gray-headed men who appeared to enlarge every one of their facial hairs with special attention. They all came with their own distinctive words, looks, laughs, and exuberances. I got depressed amid these murky waves of people, who sometimes smelt of alcohol, sometimes of onions or pungent lavender, and looked at every face with a different type of astonishment. My reclusive mood must have caught the attentive gaze of my large-bellied guide at the other end of the *sofra* (he was busy downing what was perhaps his hundredth glass of wine) because he constantly leaned over toward me and said:

"Son, no secret remains hidden to us! I understand. You look like a philosophical man; you look at everything as a lesson. Come talk here beside me, I know how to talk philosophy too."

Some laughed with tears at this statement. As he said this, a tall, unusual-looking man entered who, wearing a cotton vest turned inside out on his back, resembled a scarecrow sticking up in the middle of an orchard or field. Everyone called out together:

"Dervish Çinari! Well, where were you? Where did you jump out from? One more philosopher for you."

This man was the dervish with large earrings that we had bumped into in the yard of the lodge towards the evening. This was the special man that not only Nigâr, but also the entire lodge joked with. However, his face did not appear appropriate for joking around with. His eyes penetrating, his lips contracted, his nose harsh, he looked at everyone's face as if he understood nothing of what was said. I imagine that there are those who find various meanings in these glances of his. Just then, an elderly woman leaned over and said in my ear:

"My son, this is a highly respected individual; he has served the lodge for twenty years. He walked three times to and from the Master Guide, that is to Haji Bektash's tomb. There is wisdom in all his words. Everything he says comes to pass. Celile does nothing without consulting him first. Even the master goes to him when he runs into a problem. That's why he was given the crown and axe. However, there is not a bit of pride in him. He cooks the food in the kitchen during the daytime and at night he sleeps in the wooden shelter that he made with his own hands in a corner of the yard. He only participates in the *muhabbet* after this hour and sometimes doesn't appear at all. Today, however, he must have come in your honor. The truth is that this is an auspicious sign for either your *musahip* or for you yourself."

The *musahip*, or spiritual companion, she mentioned would be Nigâr. As for the woman beside me with the enchanting words, let her say what she will, I felt that this night was not going to be very auspicious for Nigâr. Tonight, at this half-lush *sofra*, she was turning a rather important corner in her life. The black-bearded man beside her, riding a swelling wave of passion, was pulling her closer each moment, slowly covering her, quietly wrapping her up. I was not the only one who perceived this. Aunt Ziba pointed them out to me many times with her glances.

Both of them appeared to be detached from the group and engrossed in one another. Nur Baba was speaking constantly, laughing continually. Now and again, Alhotoz Afife interrupted their conversation, but then they continued again one-on-one. What could this frivolous dervish in a white robe possibly explain to Nigâr? How could Nigâr bear to listen to him for hours? What is the thing that unites these opposites to one another? What did this crass languidness lend to the man's eyes? What kind of joy is it that filled the woman's throat with such unrestrained laughter? Eventually, the hour came when I could no longer recognize my level-headed, innocent beloved: she was now a flirtatious, empassioned woman, intoxicated in every respect. Does the personality of every woman contain a hidden harlot in embryonic state that waits for the opportunity like this to be born?

They all began to sing again. The master's voice was heard above all others. Nigâr bowed her head and let herself drift into a state of deep ecstasy. I wanted to cry. There was something in my soul rotting, crumbling, dying bit by bit. All those frightening, black and red demons of the imperceptible world were filling my soul one by one: spite, disgust, despair, fear, shame, torment of conscience, disillusionment and legion other types of disturbances; sundry and various pains that cannot be placed, which cannot be named: jealousy, rage, feelings of revolt. I was brimming with all of these. I felt that my life and my existence had been an absolute tragedy. I was probing the depths of melancholy. Right at this moment an important event occurred: Aunt Ziba and

Nasib began to fight in an indescribable manner. According to some, this fight arose from the line of a hymn that was being sung:

> *This is a morsel of resignation,*
> *didn't I say you couldn't eat it?*[13]

The mischievous Nasib had yelled this line several times with a loaded, mocking tone at Aunt Ziba's face and, while pointing at the master with her eyes, made such unbearable insinuations that Aunt Ziba erupted. I had never seen her this terrifying. She was like a leopard foaming at the mouth, ready to pounce on her prey; she rose up on two knees, her eyes leapt out of their sockets, her body trembled, and she shouted with all her strength:

"I ate, I ate, I ate, I digested and I even spit it out. If you want some, I'll give you some of my leftovers! Don't worry! He can feed hundreds of hungry and voracious people like you! For years, hundreds of hungry people like you."

Nasib continually repeated the same line with unrestrained laughter and, as she did so, Aunt Ziba lost control of herself. A moment came in which this heated argument showed the potential of becoming a wild wrestling match; one woman's hands were looking for things to throw at the other's head, the other was standing up and preparing to attack. Nur Baba, on one side, and Rauf, on the other, prevented this catastrophic contingency, and Aunt Ziba was restrained with difficulty. Thankfully, before long, a crisis of nerves overtook them both. Nasib's plump body fell into Rauf's lap, sobbing; Aunt Ziba collapsed beside the *sofra* crying hoarsely and trembling violently like a tigress that had become the victim of a sudden arrow shot in the middle of her chest. But it was not over. One part of the crowd huddled around Nasib's side, the other gathered around the twisiting, writhing body of Aunt Ziba, and a tiresome squabble broke out between those who were fainting and those who ran to revive them. Only Celile, Dervish Çinari, and I remained observers. The white-haired woman stood with spiteful, contemptuous indifference. The dervish with large earrings was amazed as if he were beholding a miracle. Those who were strewn about the room a bit earlier had been woken by the commotion, and dizzily turned their clouded faces, their wretched heads from the shadows and around the edges of the *sofra*, toward the light. As for me, I was thinking about going to bed. Maybe a bit later, I too would pass out where I sat; my head was heavy and my stomach was upset. I approached Celile, who still stood in the same manner, and said:

"Could you please show me where I'm going to sleep?"

She laughed. "I guess you drank a lot of booze, son."

---

13 A line from the poem *Demedim mi* by the famous sixteenth-century Kızılbaş-Alevi bard Pir Sultan Abdal. It came to be used in Bektaşi ceremonies as a *nefes*.

As I got up, I felt that the place where I stood was shaking and saw those around me as if they were behind a cloud. What happened last night after this point remains a half-dream for me.

Though I remember such an event, I still don't know very well whether it really happened or if it was just a nightmare lodged in my inebriated brain.

My head was sticking out of a high window, vomiting toward the cool darkness. Beside me a woman that I clearly perceived to be Nigâr held one hand on my forehead while the other was squeezing a wet cloth on my hair. I pulled her hand toward my lips several times and moaned, "Oh, Nigâr Abla! Nigâr Abla!" and began to cry. Nigâr said:

"Oh, Macid, oh my brother. Wake up, collect yourself a bit."

I don't know how long this situation continued. I saw Nur Baba suddenly approach us, take Nigâr by her waist, slowly pull her toward him, and then the two of them disappeared into the darkness, whispering.

At this moment, as I write these lines, I am hoping that this was nothing but a nightmare, not only this but everything related to last night...

The last twenty-four hours exhausted me to the root of my existence, as if I had lived through a hundred-year adventure. There are numerous burdens of memory piled, heavy and black, on my head. Where had I been? Where had I come from? Had I been to the palace of dissolute Persian royalty? Had I participated in the entertainments of a flippant Turkish prince? In which historical era, in what part of the world was I? However, I think that, from one angle, last night's entertainment was neither extraordinarily revolting, nor excessively catastrophic so as to leave such a profound impression on me. Actually, the fecund panorama of humanity in which every individual entered an ebullient wave of passion—shouting, laughing, crying, fainting, writhing, passing out in that dimly lit place that half-resembled a temple—was, for me, one of life's most unusual scenes. It contained a tragic expression of humanity that was incomplete, rotten, crippled, and meek. And the man called Nur Baba was the first unique and bizarre specimen I had seen of the country where I had grown up. This man, who was passionate from head to toe, pure appetite from top to bottom, was busy stirring a demonic cauldron that boiled many souls on a stove whose fire never extinguished, like the sorcerers in the medieval fairy tales, all in a quiet corner of Istanbul.

From now on, I'll never see Nigâr again...

8 The Second Period of Guidance

Within a month of the night Nigâr took initiation, she visited Nur Baba's lodge twice more.

However, during this period, neither a day nor a night passed in which she didn't see Nur Baba or stayed far from him. As a matter of fact, the very first night after the Ceremony of Union—towards midnight, the young woman heard Nur Baba's voice outside her bedroom as she lay in bed with shivers and goose bumps all over her body. When she looked out the window toward the sound, the black-bearded Sufi guide sang from a long rowboat in the middle of the cove in a half-lit, silent night:

...Oh, breeze, don't blow while my beloved is asleep[1]

She heard him belt out a song with a voice that went up and down note by note. A pleasant fear covered her entire body, her knees trembled, and she fell to the floor where she stood.

The following afternoon she was going into town. Just as she was about to hop from the dock onto the ferry, she saw that Nur Baba was walking right beside her. She was accompanied by her oldest child and the child's nanny, a loyal elderly servant. Given the shock, she almost left them, turned around, and ran back to the mansion. She suddenly became so dizzy that she gave way at the knees.

The black-bearded, black-turbaned Sufi master did not leave her trail that day until evening; they got off the ferry side-by-side. In the Beyoğlu neighborhood, they had wandered around all of the stores as if they were together. Nur Baba sometimes became invisible among the people, other times he followed from quite a distance; sometimes he suddenly popped out right in front of them, and now and then he walked step-by-step behind the young woman. Nigâr went through the day in a trancelike state.

---

1 From a poem by Abdülhamid Ziyâeddin better known as Ziya Pasha (1829–80):

Ey sabâ esme nigârım uykuda
Sevdiğim çeşm-i humârım uykuda
Değme lûtfet gül'izârım uykuda...

DOI: 10.4324/9781003381471-9

Her feet stumbled over one another as she walked, when she stopped she became dizzy, and when she felt Nur Baba very close, she very nearly choked from the pounding of her heart. As they entered the store *Au Lion*[2] to buy clothes for the child, he passed beside her so closely that their shoulders touched on the narrow stairway, and the nanny said, "What is this dervish's problem? Wherever I go, he jumps out in front of me!" Nigâr almost rolled down the steps upon hearing that; she turned angrily to the woman and growled, "Shut up, Peyker, my dear! You can't tell the house from the street! It's useless to go anywhere with you anyway," and quickly went outside and threw herself into a carriage. When she arrived home, she was a nervous wreck. She still felt the black-bearded master behind her and kept shivering at the thought of him. At night, she said to herself a few times: "Oh, how persistent, how dangerous this man is!" Her mind was completely empty, but in her soul there was the angry, spiteful, and painful reality of a woman who had been obtained by force. She thought of writing an angry letter to abort this escapade, which was beginning to become distasteful, and to teach him some manners. However, she didn't do this and, two days later, she was again face to face with him.

It was truly a bizarre coincidence. Nasib had come to visit her in the afternoon. In the house, Nigâr managed to keep her companion for an overnight visit by insisting and begging, and, late in the evening, they went out to stroll in the surrounding countryside. They passed by the wooded part on the hill beside the mansion and walked slowly up a narrow goat trail that climbed a small green hill. There were thorny, fragrant, small natural hedges on both sides of the trail. The air was light and full of a bitter aroma. Nigâr kept her hands busy with the sides of her head scarf as she talked again to her companion about Nur Baba, for perhaps the tenth time. Concerning Nur Baba, the young woman spoke words that expressed sometimes shock, sometimes anger, and other times fear. Actually, Nur Baba's sudden emergence out of the sea for a nocturnal serenade outside the windows of the mansion was an event that had left her awestruck. And wasn't it the morning of the same day that Nigâr had left Nur Baba in a corner of Çamlıca in a state of exhaustion and misery perhaps as extreme as her own?

Despite this, how did it happen that in the evening of the same day he had found the strength and energy to take off from the shores of Üsküdar and come as far as the Kanlıca cove?[3] Where in the vicinity did he spend

---

2 See Map II. The full name of the store was *Au Lion d'Or* located at 338 & 340 Grande Rue de Pera (Cadde-i Kebir or today's İstiklal Caddesi). It specialized in silk and wool products. "Bonmarşeler" *Dünden Bugüne İstanbul Ansiklopedisi*, 297. For more on European department stores in Istanbul, see: Yavuz Köse, "Vertical Bazaars of Modernity: Western Department Stores and Their Staff in Istanbul (1889–1921)," *International Review of Social History* 54, no. 17 (2009): 91–114.

3 The distance from the ferry dock of Üsküdar to the dock of Kanlıca is approximately 11km/ 6.8miles.

the night? How did he arrange the coincidence on the dock of Kanlıca the following day? How did he know that Nigâr would go into Istanbul that day at that hour? There was almost the inkling of a miracle in each of these feats of the young master. Since Nasib was a fervently believing Bektashi, she considered all these things as quite natural for a Sufi master and, in plain speech, was telling her companion about the mysterious powers held by outstanding souls like him, their dizzying manifestations, and the divinity of love.

Afterward, Nigâr said that these recent activities of Nur Baba did not sit well with her. If everything were limited to the run-in on the dock, fine, but the persistent stalking in Beyoğlu, she found appropriate neither to the exaltedness of the Path nor to the office of the Sufi leader and, while thinking of it in this way, she felt the half-sincere, half-contrived need to appear a bit angry in front of her companion.

"No matter what you say...this man is too wild, too shameless. I've had a rotten conscience for the past three days, as if I had committed a sin. I feel regret. I'm frightened," she said.

It was right then, at a turn on the narrow path behind the crumbling fountain wall, that Nur Baba suddenly leapt into view. The hem of his robe, the bottom of his trousers, and his shoes were covered in dust and mud, his face was sweating and had turned pale, and his chest was heaving. Nasib recoiled two steps; she pressed her thumb behind her front teeth and yelped "Ah, Ah, Ah!" a few times.

His disciple froze and remained still. She looked around for a place to rest.

"Do not fear, my lady, it's me. Do not fear!" the master said.

He began to wipe his forehead with a wide cream-colored handkerchief made of silk. He appeared to have come quite a long way. After he said, "Do not fear," the two young women looked at each other with bewilderment. With a shock that gradually increased, Nasib examined the disheveled dervish across from her and said:

"We are at a loss for words, Master! I don't know what to make of you."

Nigâr was silent and felt that her words were bunched up in her throat like knots.

Nur Baba answered Nasib with a trembling voice:

"I don't know either...Ask the lady about it. I don't know!"

Nigâr laughed with an indecipherable, forced smile and looked ahead. Motioning with his hand to the fresh disciple, the master repeated:

"Ask the lady about it."

With a flirtatious laugh, Nasib said:

"Oh, what would she know, Master? For the love of God, drop the joke; where are you coming from, how did you come? Our..."

The young man interrupted her a second time:

"I don't know, don't ask in vain, I don't know."

Only after this did Nigâr suddenly feel the need to get a word in:

"His Sainthood is right, Nasib," she said. "For three or four days, he hasn't known what to do with himself."

The young woman said this in a half-rebuking, half-mocking manner.

However, Nur Baba seemed oblivious to this snide remark. He laughed and said:

"Did you see? She said I was right."

From his looks and laughing, they understood that he was a bit tipsy. He stayed with them until a late hour and wouldn't leave without them promising to come to the lodge the following day.

The following day, Nigâr went to the lodge alone. Actually, she had insisted to her female companion that they go together as she couldn't find the courage to go on this kind of casual visit alone. The stretches of roads between Kanlıca and Çamlıca frightened her. Especially the thought that she would come face-to-face with Nur Baba alone conjured in her nocturnal imagination the image of a deep, dark well, of the kind found in fairy tales, filled with legions of multi-headed dragons. If nothing else, she wanted to bring someone from the house with her, but after giving it some thought, she gave up. She thought that going to Madame Ziba might be more appropriate, but for whatever reason, she could not find the courage for this either.

When she got off the ferry at the Üsküdar dock, Alhotoz Afife came to mind, as the last resort. She knew that this elderly woman resided in a large, old mansion in Sultantepe and so to Sultantepe she went; however, she found the heavy door with the knocker locked up securely. When she returned to her carriage alone, she didn't know where to go or what to do and wallowed in despair and indecision. An anger with no clear cause or target raged inside her; she repeatedly put on her gloves and took them off, lifted her veil and put it down. After all, wasn't serving and helping each other one of the principles of the Bektashi order? They had left her all alone on her very first step of the path. It was Nasib who had brought things to this point, who more or less created this visit, and she was also the first to abandon her. Nigâr was a bit angry at Nur Baba as well. For which reason and by what right had he called her to his side? After a few successful conquests like Madame Ziba, this man had lost control of himself; he was nothing more than a conceited egotist who fancied that he had the right to possess every woman.

Upon having this thought, she ordered the driver back to the dock. "*No, I'm not going to go, no.*" she said to herself. What had happened up until now had happened. Being part-bored, part-curious, and part-stubborn she had acted in an unimaginably strange way; part-bored, part-stubborn, part-curious, she had suddenly plunged her life, which had resembled a crystal wine glass full of colorless, odorless but clear liquid, into fetid water and pulled it out, and, because of this, she felt a perverse pleasure. However if adventure was necessary, this much had been sufficient. Inside herself, she said, "I'm in control, am I not? I can turn back whenever I choose. I'm in control, right?" But when she arrived at the Üsküdar dock, a small event reversed the young woman's train of thought. The ferry that followed the Anatolian shore had just taken off and the next boat required more than an hour-and-a-half wait. Though Nigâr decided to wait, she found this stretch of time unbearable, and it reminded her of every moment of her life, each as long as an epoch, full of empty, heavy hours. She saw herself inside the large, old waterside mansion where she was born, raised, and married; her hands were empty, her eyes were empty, her mind was empty, sometimes wandering from one room to the other, sometimes laying face down on her *chaise longue*, sometimes filling the empty, bottomless mouth of the woodstove, which had not been in use since the winter, with continually and involuntarily smoked, unfinished cigarettes. At times like these, she felt that the incessant, silent, and gnawing cycle of the chain inside the clock rotated around her heart. From behind the forged iron grill of the ferry station's waiting room, Eşref Pasha's wife looked out at the pale waters of Üsküdar's shoreline and her chest fell and rose several times with slow, labored breaths.

At this moment, no life disaster could have been as painful and heart-wrenching as this dreadful inner distress that caused her chest to swell. She looked at her watch over and over, again and again, and said to herself: "There're still forty-five minutes, *forty-five minutes!*" Murmuring this to herself, she slowly went outside and gave up on going home. A half-hour later, Nigâr was in the lodge of Nur Baba.

His eyes full of joy, the young master greeted her at the door of the garden. The female disciples waved their white hankerchiefs from the windows. The young woman quickly felt at ease with the crowd of the lodge and said to Nur Baba:

"Oh, how nice! There is no shortage of guests here. I had supposed that we would be alone tonight."

The young master listened to these words with a happy and rather suggestive smile. "What can I do, my lady? Lodges are always like this. Always," he said.

Nigâr saw no need to explain what she meant to say. Within a minute, the liveliness and lightness had settled upon her, from head to toe. She exchanged a prolonged greeting with Celile who waited for her in front of the door, joked with a few of the disciples, laughing together and emitting sweet fragrances around her. Then she went up to undress in the room that was being prepared for her. Nur Baba glanced sidelong at an old disciple standing beside him, took a deep breath and spoke slowly, "Atiye, God knows that I am intoxicated…"

Was there much drinking that night? Because there were no instruments, Nur Baba sang. Nigâr got so drunk that the next day she couldn't get herself together until evening and could only return to the waterfront mansion on the last ferry. Her children had already gone to bed and her mother was waiting at the top of the stairs for her, worried and angry. The elder woman greeted her daughter with a sulking face:

"By God, this is outrageous, Nigâr! You didn't think of us, but only yourself. How could you stay out so late without getting afraid?" she said.

Nigâr was in no condition to remain standing. Laughing, she extended her cheek to her mother and immediately took refuge in her room.

As for the next day, she stayed in bed until evening and only managed to stand up with difficulty at a late hour to meet with an elderly woman who came to visit her. The identity of this woman was completely unknown to the people of the house. However, Nigâr recognized her instantly and took her into her room. The visitor came from the lodge. She had been sent by Nur Baba particularly to inquire after her health and had also brought a letter in her bosom. This letter discussed love, longing, meeting, and the agony caused by separation. Upon leaving, the elderly woman said, "He definitely wants a response to this."

Sir Safa's granddaughter laughed and said:

"You can see that I'm not feeling so well, my hands are shaking and my head is spinning. Tell him this."

Two days hadn't passed when a second letter from Nur Baba came to Nigâr. From start to finish, it was replete with rebukes and complaints; the crazy-hearted master opened:

> *The one I worship has an appearance that is pleasant but a character that is cruel. Why do you see fit to inflict such injustice upon on your admirer? With the groaning winds, my nights have been confused with my days and my days with my nights. Days that pass by without you are no different from the night of the winter solstice, the longest of the year. The food I eat sticks in my throat like knots. The wine I drink enters my body like a lethal poison. One by one, every part of my body cries out for you. I am beginning to dread myself. You are my prayer niche; to you I turn, and from you I seek my cure.*

After many complaints, he closed with:

> *On your last visit, you prevented your wretched beloved from strolling around you. I obeyed because for me your orders are sacred on the same level as divine commands. I gritted my teeth; for four days now, I have not disturbed you with my presence. Is it too much to ask that you reciprocate this sacrifice of mine with a token of grace? My lady, what if you would indulge to inquire after the welfare of my miserable self. If you would only sprinkle a bit of hope and cheer in my heart! Your response last time said "I can't write, because I'm not feeling well", etc.*

After the letter ended, the woman messenger, Atiye began:

"Every day, every hour, he talks about you. Sadly, he let himself go again. He immerses himself in thought at the head of the dinner table, then leaves rapidly, isolates himself in a corner, and cries. At midnight, the wine bottles disappear under his armchair. Poor Celile is in a state of shock. If it weren't for her, the state of the lodge would be dire. However, it is known, my girl, that the disciple comes for the master. How will Celile fill in for him? Anyhow, the cautious woman doesn't exhibit her weakness. She doesn't, but still, it can't go on like this, for two reasons. First, her patience will run out, and after it has...Oh, bless her; she keeps her patience as much as possible. She is actually a patient woman, but I don't know how long a person can be patient in circumstances like these. This idea of age and appearance being irrelevant for love, my dear. Maybe you have been blunting your desires for a long time, but one day you will be surprised to see that..."

Nigâr laughed. Atiye opened up even more, with an overly familiar voice:

"Don't laugh, my dear, don't laugh. A heart is God's house. This is nothing to joke about. Oh, this youth! Oh, this ignorance. People suppose that *muhabbet* is amusement, a romp, laughing at one another. I love you, you love me, meaningful gifts, scented letters. Well, this is what those at your age understand from *muhabbet*. The good old *muhabbet*. *Muhabbet*. My dear, the *muhabbet* that we know—may God protect you from it—is something like an earthquake, a lightning bolt, a conflagration, a flood, a curse, a catastrophe. I don't wish a fate like this upon you, but let me say this: avoid enabling any sin."

The elder woman was unable to achieve her purpose. Nigâr—with her special smile that combined sarcasm, pride, and insolence—aided her conversation partner:

"Ok, madame, I understand," she said, "but what do you want me to do? In what manner do you want me to behave?"

"It's not like that, my dear. It isn't my place to show you the way; but by God, the state of Celile and the lodge due to Nur Baba's condition distressed me. It perturbed me and drove me to open up to you like this. Perhaps if the master hears about how much I shared, he would not be pleased. My lamb, keep this between you and me. Let me keep on as if I had known nothing. Please write a reply to the letter."

Nigâr pondered for a while and finally wrote these few lines:

> *If I had not known you very well and from up close, your letter might have saddened me greatly.* Muhabbet *is your art and not even you can transgress its limits. Please don't expect very much from me. I will come and see you once in a while. I implore you with complete respect.*

This was the first thing that Nigâr had ever written pertaining to *muhabbet*. After giving the page to the elder woman, she admired her own courage as if she had performed an important task, and a feeling akin to regret awakened in her heart. Already for the past few months, either disenchantment, fear, or regret followed her every action. At the root of her identity resided an inauspicious premonition that slithered like a black snake from time to time. She imagined herself to be exposed to a disaster at every moment. However, these episodes did not last long. All the darkness of her soul melted and disappeared in a momentary fit of joy. Thus, before Nur Baba's skilled disciple-messenger with the letter in her pocket had crossed the threshold leaving the house, the granddaughter of Sir Safa entered her room smiling, flirtatious, and aflame. She opened the letter that had been stuffed into the side of the armchair she sat in earlier. She approached the window; for a long time, she read the letter over and over. It gave her a sense of wonder as if it were the first thing she had ever seen in her life, or the first word she had ever heard. A silent pleasure filled her heart as she found every word particularly familiar and intimate. Because in Nigâr—as in all women—every manifestation of love emerged from natural desires, and the letter was addressed precisely to these desires. After her eyes sucked in every sentence with a profound appetite, craving satiation, she folded the page and, as if she could not find place in her room worthy of preserving it, she slowly inserted it in her bodice. For a time, she remained dreamy and entranced. She felt sorry for Nur Baba as the cold reply she sent was in cruel contradiction to the fire of his letter.

Nur Baba also found it as such, and because of this, he came by boat to the window of Nigâr during the following night to complain with his strong, burning voice from the sea.

It was not as late as the last time. There were still a couple of hours until midnight.

Nigâr had fallen into a family conversation in the royal salon adjoining her own bedroom with her cousins, mother, and Macid, who had come as guests the day before from the Şişli district of Istanbul to the waterfront mansion. Macid, despite his decision not to see Nigâr, still came by the house once in a while. They were in the midst of enjoying one of the ultra-thin cigarettes that they smoked, one after the other, during the time of digestion after dinner.

Suddenly her entire body was covered in chills, and in the middle of a discussion, she stopped talking two or three times with her eyes opened wide, her eyebrows raised and excitedly and attentively listened to what was going on outside. This behavior of the young woman was so spontaneous and apparent that everyone noticed. Aside from Nigâr's cousins who were equipped with a sensitivity that was more acute than necessary and Macid who was feverishly jealous and devoted at least three out of five of his senses to observe the perceptible and imperceptible manifestations of her presence, even Nigâr's mother, who appeared to have entered another world with her own preoccupations in a corner of the room, noticed her state and said:

"What happened to you all of a sudden?"

Like a child caught in the act, Nigâr had no idea what to say; she was stunned and froze. She decided to save herself from this problematic situation with a response that was only clear to herself but required additional explanation for those in the room.

"Don't you hear? Someone is singing a serenade in the bay."

At once, everyone involuntarily drew near the window and listened. Only Macid remained where he sat. Now he heard the voice at sea clearly and understood very well whose voice it was and what it meant. The cousins wanted to turn down the lamps and open one of the lattice-work windows. Nigâr said,

"Leave it, please. Come and sit down. So excited over this! Didn't you ever hear a song on the sea before?"

"But Nigâr, this is something completely different. It's an exceptional voice," they replied.

Safa Efendi's elder daughter-in-law, Nigâr's mother, also joined the side of the young girls.

"It really is a burning and moving voice," she said.

The windows opened quickly and Nur Baba's tones overcame the silent, half-dark salon like rushing waves. The master of *muhabbet* sang like this:

> *Love with your soul the one who says that he loves you with all his life*
> *After all, it is to love and be loved that feeds the soul*

At times the voice lowered in profound moans, sometimes it rose in impassioned exclamations, and long tremorous silences followed the harmony of every verse. In the silence, the heads sticking out of windows only listened to the gentle sounds of the rowboat as it drew closer to them with the movement of the waves. Nigâr pulled back from the window and slowly sat down in the darkness beside Macid. Then, Macid leaned over to her and said in a slow, but bitter and sarcastic, voice:

"Nigâr, congratulations. You've made progress with him!"

Nigâr froze up. Her teeth chattered as if just getting out of a dip in the sea, and the root of her being trembled.

Macid repeated, "Congrats, congrats."

The young woman didn't have the strength to respond. She could only feel the bitter accusation of her companion and haltingly begged:

"Be quiet, Macid. Don't you see that I'm in pieces? I'm suffocating."

It was as if Nur Baba's voice gradually came closer. Actually, the young master, who was a bit drunk, had instantly sensed the opening of the windows. He thought that it was a favorable sign to him and began to row his boat slowly toward the mansion. As the boat approached the house, stroke by stroke, his voice lowered by degrees, with quivering tones, and then harmonious sobs and ardent wailing overcame him.

Macid said sarcastically:

"What an eloquent 'serenade'." After deliberating for a moment, leaning even closer to Nigâr, with the same voice, he added these caustic words, "But what a shame that the lover has no lute and the beloved has no sense of coquetry." The young woman bit her lips and murmured as if speaking to herself:

"Let's hope that he doesn't come any closer, any closer…"

"Did you really encourage him *this much*?" Macid asked.

Now the voice outside had ceased, but it felt as if the rowboat had come right in front of the windows. Nigâr's mother suddenly pulled her head inside and said:

"Oh! It's a very unseemly man."

She signaled to her nieces to close the lattice windows. Nigâr tried to laugh and said something like, "Heavens! Close the curtains too and let's turn on the lamps."

The master of *muhabbet* began singing a lament from the sea that rose step-by-step and slowly began to depart:

> *The fire of my cry illuminates the path of union.*
> *In order to prove that you are a slave of the sons of the Lion,*[4]
> *That moon-faced beauty presents Nuri with the chalice of suffering.*

Nigâr couldn't sleep at all that night. A persistent, unceasing rage boiled throughout her being. But against whom? For what? Until morning, she herself couldn't distinguish this.

At dusk, an older woman sent by Nur Baba whom Nigâr didn't know at all, came to visit. This woman's style was elegant, her voice soothing, and her eyes full of enigma. With a familiar and friendly posture, she approached Nigâr and said secretively:

"My diamond, I'm not a stranger. I'm one of the children of Nur Baba, his first child you might say."

The young woman took her guest into a small dark room decorated in dark red velvet. This place was a corner of privacy, free from all the sounds of the waterfront mansion. The two disciples sat close together in deep armchairs, facing one another. The lady guest was in that state of hesitation particular to those who do not know where to begin a conversation. On her face, which was softened and weathered by who knows what strange gusts of wind, there were fresh, innocent, bashful shadows that were similar to those on a young girl. Nevertheless, her eyes harbored a hidden interest in prying. After glancing over her surroundings several times, she finally said:

"I'm very sorry that I didn't attend the Gathering Ceremony you attended, and afterward there hasn't been a good chance to meet. Anyway, I haven't been going to the lodge for some time. But we are very close to one another; I live just there in Anadolu Hisarı. The master, may God bless him, forgives me and still comes to visit me often because I am the first of his disciples. His inclination toward me is excessive. But the *muhabbet* for his most recent disciple is more than for any other..."

She couldn't finish her sentence and laughed. Nigâr behaved as if she didn't understand. Nur Baba's first child continued:

"Recently, the frequency of his visits to me has been because of you, and I am indebted to you for this happiness. The need to be as close as possible to you drives him to my humble abode once every two or three days. All he does is circumambulate your house, sometimes by sea, sometimes by land during the night. This is really a very dangerous game both for himself and for you..."

---

4 The Lion ("Haydar") refers to Ali. His sons ("slave of the sons") are Hasan and Husayn.

Kanlıca is the size of your palm. There is no one around who doesn't know this house. As for the master, there's no need to go on at length, my dear! The crown of Husayn that he wears says it all…"[5]

Nigâr cut her interlocutor short:

"How nice, Madame, you're saying everything that I'm thinking and everything that I would say! Everything that I have said to him time and time again."

"In that case, I implore you. Find a solution to this! Since last night I have been out of my mind. My girl, tell me about last night. What have you done to him?"

Right at this moment, coffee was brought for the guest. The instant the servant stopped in front of the door with the tray in hand, Nigâr could barely contain herself from curiosity and felt as if she would die from impatience.

After Nur Baba's first child drank her coffee, she lit a cigarette and waited until the servant had completely departed. Nigâr said:

"For goodness sake, Madame, what happened last night? What have I done? Do tell!"

The lady guest let out a long sigh, and said:

"Last night? God forbid, don't ask. Last night was a night of disaster, both for him and for me. He returned in such a state from that rowboat joyride that I thought, oh God forbid, that he had either lost his mind or was about to die. He was soaking wet from head to toe and completely miserable. His turban was unwound and every button on his jacket had popped off. Bare-chested, his hair and beard tangled together, his eyes bulging out of their sockets. He didn't have the strength to stand, much less walk. After entering in this state, he leaned against the door and remained motionless and silent in the room for a long while. I was at a loss as how to respond and nearly lost my mind. The lamp in my hand clanged because I was trembling. He looked blankly at my face, as if seeing me for the first time. He appeared as if he wanted to say something, to cry out, and as he did this, his chest and throat swelled with moans. I wanted to take him inside, put him somewhere comfortable, but this was impossible. The moment he moved slightly from his place, faltered in his steps, and fell headfirst onto the stones. At that point, I had absolutely no idea what to do. If I had awoken my servant, it wouldn't have done any good. I couldn't bear the idea of someone seeing him in this state…God gave me fortitude. I put down the lamp in my hand, bent over, and passed my hands underneath his arms and dragged him to the bed. My dear, imagine me carrying him, how can such a thing happen? Well, it did. Just as other similar things have occurred by the strength of the master and the strength of the faith…"

---

5 The crown or "*tac*" of Hussein is a special kind of Bektashi headgear. It is made of felt and has twelve pleats that symbolize the Twelve Imams. The name *fahr-ı Hüseyin*, or literally the Glory of Husayn, refers to the grandson of Prophet Muhammad and son of Ali and Fatima, who died at Karbala. The headgear is commonly known as the "*Hüseyni tac*."

Nigâr was obliged to listen to her ramblings and other tales about the strength of this master and the power of faith. Her patience waned as her guest digressed while she was about to get to the crux of the matter at hand. Several times, she wanted to say, "What happened to him? Explain this and that. What happened to him?" The disciple from Anadolu Hisarı returned to the original subject sometime later, as evening approached and the velvety room filled with shadows.

"I placed him in the bed," she said. "But don't imagine that everything ended there. The real catastrophe began after this. Powerful shivers overcame his entire body as if the bed were a block of ice. I had wet his head with cold water and thought that it began afterward. Immediately, I dried him and wrapped him up with whatever I could find. With all my strength, I began to knead and massage his body, but it was futile. The shaking gradually increased, and his teeth chattered as if they were going to break. I understood that it wasn't an ordinary chill. It required a different cure. But what cure could I find? Where could I go in the middle of the night? I was pacing back and forth in the room calling out, 'Oh my *pir*, come to my aid!' A bit later, the shaking stopped, but Master's condition entered a more disturbing state. His teeth locked up, his fists clenched tightly, his neck became rigid, his back arched, his entire body tightened like drawn bow, he tossed about under the comforters with a bitter voice and even curled up in the corner of the room. I lost it. For some time I could not gather the courage to approach him. I froze up. Then I realized that this wouldn't do. He tossed himself about, here and there, bumping his head and arms. I drew near, threw myself on top of him, pressed my knees on his shoulders, and held his arms down with all the strength I could muster. It was futile, my dear, futile! Never mind controlling him, I could barely control myself! Good Lord! In fact, he is very strong and imposing, but in this situation he became something entirely different. It was as if he became iron—no, better yet, a lion, from head to toe, an enraged lion, Madame. Look here, completely bruised," said Nur Baba's first child, pulling up the sleeves of her blouse to show her elbows and wrists. They were covered in black bruises. "If you saw my shoulders and knees, you would feel even worse for me. But could I think of myself at that time? Where was I? Was I on the floor? Was I in the sky? I had completely forgotten."

Nigâr interrupted the visitor from Hisar and said:

"According to what you've explained, Master must have experienced an episode of hysteria. How strange, I thought that this illness was particular to women."

The disciple slowly continued speaking, closing her eyes lightly with a suggestive smile:

"Say whatever you want, my love. Maybe this isn't a malady that can be named easily, and it does not discriminate between male and female. Actually, I too faint and have seen many who faint and come to, as it happens to almost everyone in the lodges. However, my dear, the condition I have explained is something completely different, extraordinary, beyond anything seen or heard. I don't know how to explain it. I would not wish this state upon you. However, I am certain that if you had seen this with your own eyes at that instant, without hesitation, you would have sacrificed everything, your whole life, to that man who writhed, flailed about, and slammed his head into a wall for you."

The woman looked into Nigâr's eyes and finished the story:

"Morning came. He opened his eyes, hiccupping and crying. He was calling out 'Nigâr, Nigâr, Nigâr!' and tearing at his chest with his nails. Yet how right he was in this agony! As he explained the events of the previous night, one by one, I too began to cry involuntarily. With a thousand hopes, wishes, and desires, he sang to your window from afar on the sea. His only intention was to look at the light in your window, and, even if you were not in that light, to at least be able to see one of your shadows and then pull back and leave. However, you encouraged him beyond these expectations. You raised the lattice windows and did several things to imply that you did not object to his coming closer. After this, he slowly came toward you—there is no need to say the rest I suppose. You closed the windows and said, 'What an unseemly man!'"

Here Nigâr interrupted her interlocutor.

"Wrong, Madame. He either misinformed you or didn't hear correctly and misunderstood."

She provided a long, detailed explanation about that night and what happened in front of the window.

As she explained, the guest from Hisar examined her, squinting her eyes with a gradually increasing scrutiny, and her mind appeared to be occupied with other things. As she stood up and departed, she said:

"Anyway, my dear, definitely go see him tomorrow."

The inside of the waterfront mansion had become dark. The chandelier in the hall had just been lit. Nigâr did not sense its dim light much. For a long spell, she remained absorbed, daydreaming in a kind of anxious happiness. Nur Baba, the dangerous and relentless lover of Aunt Ziba, and at whose knees scores of women—young and old—had bowed down, trembling passionately; Nur Baba, the master of *muhabbet*, this very man was now wallowing in abasement and agony for her. This was Nur Baba! Nigâr thought, "Yet what am I? What an immense, dangerous force I am!" and regretted the first years of her youth, which were characterized by a barren, dry outlook on and lack of zest for life. Nevertheless, the season of great romance in life had not yet passed for her. Thinking in this way, she slowly entered her room and, the next day, until she went to Nur Baba's side, her imagination knew no bounds.

Nur Baba lay sick. His face was twice as yellow and his eyes were twice as red than usual. He spoke with a heavy, angry voice and behaved contemptuously, like a spoiled child, as female disciples circulated around him, one massaging his feet, one straightening his pillows, and another handing him a variety of colorful iced drinks every other minute.

Those at the lodge received Nigâr coldly. Even Celile was all insults and mocking. The young sisters, who usually ran laughing to the door of the yard to greet her, only helped her undress with an air of cold detachment on this occasion. They made her wait a long time in an adjacent room before entering Nur Baba's quarters. Sir Safa's grandaughter felt the insult. However, she obviously didn't understand the reason for this treatment. She felt embarrassed, perplexed, and miserable.

As she came to Nur Baba and bent toward his bed in supplication, she felt disoriented. Her ears hummed, and her heart pounded with such force that it felt as if it would break her chest. Inside the room, she found a seat with some difficulty and, for a long time, could not look at anyone in the face. Nor did she find the strength to say a word, and, with her head bent over, she appeared to be busy taking off her gloves.

For a while, Nur Baba remained silent and motionless, his eyes closed, his jaw shrunken. He possessed a spiritual and otherworldly greatness in this condition. With his dark black beard and long, gaunt, pale face he resembled the mummy of an Assyrian emperor. Facing this cold, harsh display by the master of *muhabbet*, Nigâr felt a mixture of anger and fear, and wanted to sob and thrash about like a small child in the middle of the room.

Thankfully, this posturing by Nur Baba didn't last long. He raised his eyelids slightly and signaled to Mother Celile, who was sitting on the edge of the bed, and a few other disciples, to go outside. After they left, Nur Baba, looked through the eyelashes of half-open eyes, slowly turning his feeble head toward Nigâr with the grimace of an old man experiencing extreme discomfort moving and said:

"My lady, how do you like my predicament?"

Sir Safa's granddaughter turned deathly pale. After rejecting the great injustice that he wanted to blame on her with a short explanation about the previous night, and having come all the way from Kanlıca with great determination to complain about his rash behavior, excessive enthusiasm, and many other inanities that followed one after the other and multiplied—she was now faced with this question, and she suddenly didn't know what to say or do. She was silent. Her will had left her. In a strange spiritual defeat, she began to reproach herself. She felt as if her heart had been crushed with the guilt of a crime for which no amends could be made.

Nur Baba spoke:

"If your intent is to kill me, just say so! I don't fear death! But know that I don't throw myself into any fire alone. I will burn, I will roast for my *pir*, but only after reducing *you* to ash, to a pile of ashes."

The master's voice rose, his eyes opened completely and as he spoke his final words, he held out his arms and clenched his fists.

Nigâr's ears were ringing. The sick man continued his monologue:

"Now the whole lodge knows the story. Yesterday morning on my return, amid the entire group, I shouted, 'I'll make her pay for it! I will be such a scourge to her.' Now I'm saying this to your face and will say it to everyone that knows us. Let them all be witnesses. Madame, let's see what happens when you toy with a man like me! Let's see whether my heart is a child's toy like that of the well-dressed dandy Macid…"

At this point, Nigâr cut off Nur Baba's rant, her voice mixed with sobs: "Baba, you're unfair, very unfair! For God's sake, let me explain!"

Inside, she said to herself, "Oh God! He's jealous of me. He's jealous of me because of Macid," and she began to cry. However, this was an enjoyable cry. Mild-natured women like Nigâr take pleasure in crying like this. For them, every rebuke, just or unjust, every type of oppression from a man is a unquenchable grace. Their souls are fed by and flourish in the flame of torture and punishment stoked by men. The sense of retribution in them is a tame, pleasant snake that has curled up around the roots of their sex. For them, it is such a profound and universal need that, every now and then, this snake must raise its head and tickle them at a fundamental point in their being. It may be said that from the day that they are born—in their conquered, bashful hearts—these women carry the eternal sin of Eve and the eternal remorse of this sin without feeling or knowing it.

Nur Baba was by nature skilled at speaking, particularly at speaking with women, and he could, in an instant, feel what kind of a woman he was dealing with. Isn't that how he conquered the materialistic and formal Celile, like a monotonous and continuous force of nature? He played the role of a spoiled child for the proud and domineering Madame Ziba. He won over the saucy and reckless Nasib by way of telling a slew of dirty jokes and playing pranks. He seized the softspoken and pious with weeping and hymns; the elderly and the fainthearted with wine and songs, the dissolute, the corrupt, and the "experienced" with spontaneous attacks in the dark. And now, the new prey had about her the awe of a small child, in her chest the compassion of a new mother, in her facial expressions the bewildered submissiveness of a novice slave girl. He wished to make her yield to him, sometimes calling in pleasant tones, other times wailing like a sick, puny child, and in turn, with the manner of a harsh prince, wielding the sword of compulsion and oppression. As for this timid and trembling prey, she had fallen in the net some time ago. She wept partly of compassion, partly of regret, and partly out of fear, choked up and shaking in her entire being. Nur Baba sensed this and trembled with victory and pleasure like a greyhound sinking his teeth into his prey. His eyes were gleaming. However, he quickly collected himself, and, in a dignified, artificial way, said:

"You're crying. Is that so? This is another kind of torture. Are you crying to make me cry? Instead of weeping, give me an answer and say something about that dreadful night. For the love of God, say something. Deny it, lie, but say something."

The woman's sobs increased after he talked to her in this way. A bit later, she calmed down. First, she corrected Nur Baba's understanding of that night, uttering her agitated words with haste as if in rapid pursuit of something. Then she began to complain in a soft voice, not about Nur Baba but about *everything*: she complained about her life, her luck, her nature, the past and the future. As the complaints continued, the pale-faced master appeared to listen with immense, devout attention. Later, he slowly got out of the bed, drew close, grasped the hand of Nigâr that held a hankerchief soaked by her tears, and looked into the young woman's eyes with a bizarre gaze:

"My dear, surrender yourself to *muhabbet*, surrender yourself completely."

Nigâr let her head rest on the master's chest. Again, she cried profusely. Right at that moment, Celile entered the room slowly with that strange, false composure of hers.

9   Completely Smitten by *Muhabbet*

Winter in Istanbul is the season of separation and longing for lovers. It wasn't by chance that the bards sang, "Winter came, the separation inflicts wounds on my heart." However, I don't think that this verse—which is wholly Istanbulite—would express much to lovers from elsewhere because they could meet in any season and love one another, whatever the circumstance. For the people of developed and civilized capitals, winter in particular comes with parties, dances, societies, and teas. Don't first kisses happen in the corners of salons covered by thick velvet curtains and artificial plants with wide branches providing shade? As for the selected days to go to the meeting places of lovers, they particularly favored the rainy, stormy, and frigid days of winter. Because on these days, a fast-moving carriage with the windows covered tightly by curtains doesn't catch anyone's attention, and a young lover can wait for the rendezvous hour in an isolated bachelor pad, in front of a cheerfully crackling stove, laying on a long couch in complete security.

In Istanbul, in contrast, most lovers still make love in the breast of nature due to national and climatic reasons, as in folkloric tales depicting the romances of shepherds. In the popular romance here, there is a bit of rusticism. In particular, the lovers find the safest refuges and rendevous points in secluded groves, distant hills, and moonlit nights on the sea. Most of them are in the habit of revealing their secret love in songs and poems, and, usually, they go down to the waterfront in silent darkness, so that after their voices strike the intended hearer, they can disperse and disappear on the gusts of wind into the empty darkness. It may be said that, for them, nature's weather in the warm seasons and the manifestations of love complete one another; beginning and ending together, they are the two components of life with a single essence. In the period of separation, you will find in the heart of every crying lover that the desire of his beloved is mixed with the longing for a summer past. For us, every love story is more or less a history of summer.

Likewise, Nur Baba and Nigâr romanced one another for an entire summer. On the hills of Çamlıca, in the groves of the Bosphorus, on the shores of the Marmara Sea, a complete summer was filled by this passionate couple's talking, kissing, laughing, sighing, and moaning. Like first loves, they strolled freely and openly, holding hands with their chests open and heads uncovered,

DOI: 10.4324/9781003381471-10

sitting close to one another, drinking wine, and singing. They weren't bashful about anything. They found the hills so isolated, the groves so safe, and the shores so trustworthy. Sometimes other female disciples accompanied them, like Nasib, who always had their lovers with them, or like others who for some reason could not find companionship for themselves. They supposed that those around them were the guardians of their *muhabbet*. But, as fate would have it, just when Nigâr—who was completely smitten by *muhabbet*—had become a perfectly ripe fruit for Nur Baba, who was getting increasingly thirsty for her, the first rains of winter began to fall. Just like every year, this winter Nur Baba closed up the lodge and moved down to his winter residence in Üsküdar, and Nigâr moved to her husband's mansion in Nişantaşı, on the other side of the Bosphorus.[1] Aside from the problems stemming from the season and the distance that these migrations created for both of them, this separation necessitated rather significant sacrifices and created many obstacles and hardships.

Surrounded by her husband's relatives and dependents in Nişantaşı, Nigâr felt trapped inside a tight, constricting circle. Every movement was scrutinized, every word criticized, and every initiative blocked by an unseen force. From the first day of her marriage, not for a moment had her heart found peace or her body felt freedom; she could not even exercise her own free will, neither by her husband's side nor with his relatives. With them and in their circles, the young woman felt lost in another world; she was a stranger, an exile, and a prisoner.

Sir Safa's granddaughter wasn't mistaken in this feeling. Though for the last fifteen to twenty years the waterfront mansion in Kanlıca had remained closed, colorless, and silent in her father's time, it still preserved something of the exciting songs from the time of her grandfather Sir Safa, his daughter Ziba, and all those exultant voices. Together with the residence of Eşref Paşa, Ambassador to Madrid, in Nişantaşı that was even more formal and ceremonial than a consulate, the two houses formed the poles of two completely different worlds in Istanbul. In one of these worlds, there were no limits to anything; in the other, everything happened within lines that could not be crossed. At the mansion, the speech of the inhabitants was weighed, their voices were measured, their posture and their mannerisms took their final shape in front of mirrors, and the smallest movements happened according to the hour and the minute hands of the clock. As for Nigâr, who sought more of everything in life, naturally they viewed everything she did in this environment as excessive. While for her what made life beautiful, easy, and pleasurable were having confidential and warm conversations, laughing until morning, crying during songs, letting her soul be completely naked in jubilant moments, in short, of living spontaneously, openly, and joyously. Even

---

1 The real Tahir Baba Lodge in Çamlıca closed down during the winter season, only opening briefly for certain holidays: Maden, "Çamlıca'da bir Erenler Durağı," 223.

if they didn't express it openly, the fact that they secretly viewed these things as distasteful, coarse, and vulgar fostered a kind of bewilderment in her. Nur Baba's weak, gentle-hearted disciple became so depressed and miserable that she forgot even, for instance, what kind of clothing to wear at such and such hour, how such and such sentence requires you to respond in a particular manner, and how and when you could go out on the street and what time you had to be home.

Nur Baba was in no better a situation himself. His winter residence in Üsküdar was like a prison of love. Every winter, the widow known as "Nakip Pasha's wife" enclosed the master of *muhabbet* all for herself in her mansion with large halls, warmed by large tiled-wood stoves. This had been a strange relationship for Nur Baba that he had only in the winter seasons of the last three years. At first, this relationship concerned just about everyone. Led by Mother Celile and joined by Madame Ziba, all those disciples who had more intimate relations with Nur Baba than the others revolted.

Even some of the most carefree disciples protested this senseless behavior of the young master. Actually, this matter deserved revolt and protest in every which way. First, from the perspective of humaneness, it deserved protest because this winter lover was a wrinkled old woman in her seventies who couldn't get out of bed. Though she appeared to have a mother-son inter-action with Nur Baba, in fact she loved him with a jealous, selfish, and fierce passion, according to Celile. Anyhow, wasn't it proof enough of this that none of the disciples saw, heard from, or encountered the young master for the entire winter? Who had seen a leader of a Sufi order cease to perform his duties for the entire winter? For those who wanted to renew their faith, those who made a vow, those who couldn't find time to take initiation in the summer, those thirsty for long nights of ceremony and *muhabbet*, and those full of desire for divine grace and the face of God—where could they turn? Actually, there were plenty of other lodges in Istanbul, but everyone knew that those who belonged to one lodge basically had the status of a refugee when they entered another. Well, for whatever reason, it wasn't good for the children of Nur Baba to go with other *babas*. They were representatives of a different kind of Bektashi life within Bektashism and a different class of Sufi disciples. The elderly master in charge of the Sütlüce Lodge viewed Nur Baba as a heretic and couldn't refrain from hurtling insults at his children anywhere or anytime he encountered them.[2] The truth is (though, really, Nur Baba knew all of this) that it was more than negligence and nonchalance for Nur Baba's flock when he left them, even for a season, without a shepherd and in such a state of disorder; it was devastating.

---

2 Sütlüce is a district of Istanbul located on the Golden Horn. It was home to several Bektashi lodges during the late Ottoman Empire, including the Caferabad and the Karaağaç lodges. See: Fahri Maden, "Sütlüce'de bir Bektaşi ocağı: Caferabad (Bademli-Münir Baba) Tekkesi," *Alevilik Araştırmaları Dergisi* 5 (2013): 155–174.

However, when these protests began to be presented directly to him, Nur Baba, beginning with Celile and Ziba, felt the need to instruct everyone: "I'm not doing this because I enjoy it. Could you imagine what person, what soul would willingly put up with a worn-out old woman like Nakip Pasha's wife if there weren't some clear reasons for doing so? God knows, I could never bear to turn and look at her face, even for a minute. But what shall I do? The stars weren't right to open a suitable winter lodge for me. Why? Is there anyone among you who would make this sacrifice? You remain silent. Well, this woman that you dislike has promised it to me, and I'm sure that she will fulfill her vow. As her self-sacrifice and generosity are evident, every winter, I find the comfort that I never had in my own home in hers. Look at these faces," he said, motioning toward Celile and those who lived in the lodge. "She doesn't confine her grace to me only, but to each one of you, she is greatly devoted. What do you say to Çinari? Though he stays in the lodge during the winter, he's still blessed by this woman's generosity. As for Celile, she has no right to complain. She's practically ruling a mansion over there. She gets whatever she wants. You all know that I don't mind where and how I live, but nevertheless, the fact of the matter is: I have a great, a *very* great interest in this matter. The things I've ennumerated for you are minor details! There is a most essential aspect of this…"

Madame Ziba interrupted Nur Baba's last sentence with a bitter laugh and said mockingly:

"Now it's clear. Oh, what a world of hope this is! May God delay it, but death is truth, and inheriting her wealth is licit."

From this day on, the case of Nakip Pasha's wife was known among the disciples in association with the joke that "death is truth, and inheritance is licit." Nur Baba, who saw that the matter was seen this way, began to tell amusing stories about the elderly woman's rather personal, private issues, and the gatherings became carnivalesque. Nigâr, who was still quite unfamiliar with these murky, strange customs, looked at these dirty, ugly pages of the young master's life without disgust or blush of shame, nearly laughing, and once in a while contented herself with speaking to Nur Baba:

"This mysterious, passionate disciple and your lifestyle with her attracts me in the most powerful way. I have a strong desire to see this elderly beloved of yours. She reminds me of old witches in fairy tales."

However, this year, for whatever reason, Nur Baba began to find this amusing affair boring and unbearable. The passionate summer that he had spent with Nigâr had a rather significant impact on this. In the letters that the young guide occasionally sent to his new love with great difficulty, he complained:

"My forebearance is finished. I've lost my patience. Day by day, as the memory of this summer lives in me, it is becoming utterly impossible for me to submit myself to this awful winter imprisonment. My love, you should know that I'd ruin everything for a night with you, I'd destroy my future for the bliss of one more night."

At this last sentence, which was repeated in every letter, Nigâr trembled with a happy excitement and immediately responded:

"Even if you're free, I'm not. If you destroy everything, it won't fix anything. How impatient are you? How far off is summer from now?"

In reality, summer seemed like it would never arrive and, in her heart of hearts, she hoped Nur Baba would do what he said. Even if it was obvious that it wouldn't fix anything, let him destroy everything and despite its being unnecessary, let him "ruin his future" for her. Let him go so far ahead on this rocky path of *muhabbet* that it becomes a *fait accompli* for everyone such that he can't turn back. At that time, Nigâr would give her final decision, but she was already prepared to make a sacrifice, in every way imaginable.

The voice of Aunt Ziba from a year-and-a-half ago saying "imagine that you have to sacrifice quite a bit: your wealth, soul, comfort, all of these..." was always replaying in her head. Neither he nor she herself had yet to do anything resembling a sacrifice. For a year, the desire for him to enjoy her beauty and for her to enjoy his passion formed the sole basis and aim of this relationship. What is romantic love other than a Moloch fire that burns the most precious and valuable things of a person?[3] Nigâr felt this acutely and, with chills of guilt, thought about what she would throw in if the fire demanded it of her. Without a doubt, the first thing she would toss in was her husband. Next in line: her mother, her wealth, the home, and her children. This frightening vision that saddened Nigâr on these winter nights immersed her in cold sweats, and her eyelids fluttered and closed in front of these disturbing images. This was a kind of malaria of her soul; sometimes it continued at length, sometimes it came and passed, but on every occasion the young woman flew out of the room as if fleeing from a danger that crept toward her. She found her children, no matter where they were, embraced them, and then ran to her mother's side.

Macid came to the house often, but this young man who used to pour pure, cool and sweet sustenance into Nigâr's soul with his sincere, confidential conversations and sympathetic glances, now became the embodiment of regret. She always found something in his eyes that scared her, and his voice that sometimes said secretly, "You've changed so much, Nigâr Abla!" gave her the chills, like the voice of a demon of punishment and torture, and made her tremble with nightmarish imaginings for days.

Not for an instant could she raise her eyes and look at him, nor could she stay beside him for even a minute. One evening, Macid pulled her aside gently and said:

"I have some news for you. I couldn't tell you before since we couldn't be alone," he said. "I've run into our master twice in Beyoğlu. He wanders

---

3 The fire of Moloch (or alternately spelled "Molech") refers to the sacrificial offering of children to the god Moloch practiced by the ancient Israelites. In this ritual, it seems that the children were killed and then burned. The Hebrew Bible/Old Testament make numerous references to this practice, e.g., Lev. xx:2–5, Lev. xviii:21, Isa. lvii:5 and Jer. xix:5, Micah vi:7.

around from store to store, up and down the street, as if he's lost someone, with the ever-present black turban on his head, the twelve pointed head-gear, and his scraggly beard. On the first run-in, he pretended not to see me; the second time, we came so close to one another that it was impossible not to talk. But when I went beside him and greeted him with 'Master!' he was stunned. Who knows which female disciple our great master was chasing after. He complained to me saying, 'You never come by our neighborhood, what kind of discipleship is this?' he said. Then, we exchanged a few more empty words. As we went our separate ways, he asked about you. 'We never see her anymore either!' he said. I added, 'I also don't see her.'"

The young woman looked at the young man's face. It was brimming with mockery and sarcasm. The way Macid said, "I saw him. He was as if looking for someone. He asked about you. I also don't see her" had such particular, peculiar insinuations.

However, these reproachful innuendos in what Macid said that night didn't preoccupy Nigâr much. The young woman said to herself all night long: "Nur Baba definitely wants to see me." Later in the afternoon, despite everything, she had an irresistible desire to go down to Beyoğlu. At first, she went once every two days or three days, then every other day, and finally began to go every day. She would leave her carriage at the door of a store and wander on the pedestrian walks making long stops in front of the window displays. She stopped by this shop and that shop, her eyes on the outdoor displays, her hands busy with a few small pieces of clothing or fabric, in every place waiting for him. As she waited, she bought unnecessary things from every shop; some days, she was so adrift in thought that she forgot the package she bought from this store at that store, or the package of that store at this store, and returned home unbelievably exhausted. She was becoming desparate and hopeless. She thought about informing Nur Baba about her afternoon walks with a letter, but it would be like saying to him that she was waiting and looking for him in the street. And even if the encounter she so desired were to actually occur, what would happen? She didn't go out as she used to, with a male ser-vant on top of the carriage, a female servant across from her, and one of her sisters-in-law beside her. Instead, Nigâr took the children and their nanny, who appeared to bear the burden of all their needs.

However—supposing the impossible were to happen—what if one day they came face to face, for instance in the Bon Marché store?[4] Would they be able to speak? Could the possibility of this encounter be so appealing for Nigâr that she went ahead, forgetting the numerous dangers, such as encountering an acquaintance or the curious gaze of a store worker who would notice her?

---

4 A European-style store for the emerging bourgeoisie established in 1869 by the Bortoli brothers. Carrying a wide array of goods, it was particularly rich in clothing and personal items. Its ori-ginal location was the Grande Rue de Péra (Cadde-i Kabir), no. 297. Additionaly, the term "*bon marché*" came to signify a genre of European stores in Péra-Beyoğlu known in Turkish as "*bonmarşeler*": *Dünden Bugüne İstanbul Ansiklopedisi*, "Bonmarşeler," 297–298.

Figure 9.1 Au Bon Marché Store on Grande Rue de Péra. This postcard shows the Au Bon Marché store (left) in Beyoğlu on the Grande Rue de Péra (Ottoman: Cadde-i Kebir), that is today's İstiklal Caddesi.

Source: Anonymous, Courtesy of the Suna ve İnan Kıraç Vakfı Fotoğraf Koleksiyonu / Suna ve İnan Kıraç Foundation Photograph Collection, Catalog no. FKA 009361.

That's precisely how it happened. Actually, theirs wasn't an easy and surprising chance encounter of the miraculous type. As Nigâr was going down slowly to Lebon Patisserie[5] in her carriage, she saw Nur Baba in a crowd that had just come out of the Tünel funicular,[6] and this run-in made a strange impression on the young woman, as though it were a coincidence that happened years later. At first, she made some frantic involuntary motions, standing up and sticking her head out the window as if she wanted to say something to the driver. Then she suddenly froze while making these frenetic gestures, but this wasn't enough to catch the attention of Nur Baba,

5 See Map 2. The Lebon Patisserie was a famous French pâtisserie and café opened in the 1850s by either Edouard Lebon, who was previously in the service of the French Embassy, or by his son. It was an important outpost of European café culture and a meeting place for intellectuals. Well-known figures and writers such as Tevfik Fikret, Pierre Loti, Namık Kemal, Şinasi, and even Yakup Kadri Karaosmanoğlu himself were regular visitors: Nilay Kayaalp, "Pera'nın yersiz yurtsuz kahramanları: Vallauri ailesi, Edouard Lebon, Alexandre Vallauri ve M. Vedad Tek," (Unpublished dissertation, Yıldız Technical University, 2008), 34–36.
6 Tünel is an underground funicular line, one of the oldest in the world, that connects Beyoğlu and Karaköy. Designed by French engineer Eugène-Henri Gavand, it opened on January 17, 1875.

who was walking rather unaware in an unfamiliar crowd. Without turning his head, he immediately recognized to whom this slow-moving carriage belonged as he saw the woman inside out of the corner of his eye. At the same time, he sensed, of course, that he had been seen. So, he continued on his path with complete confidence. However, the carriage didn't continue down the road. After going a ways, it stopped. It appeared that it would turn off on a street, but it didn't; instead, it turned around quickly and began to race up the length of the sidewalk by Nur Baba and passed him. Vigilant and attentive from head to toe, the young guide never let the carriage out of his sight, which was reminiscent of a strange frightened creature, and he walked quickly behind it.

A bit later, on the top floor of the Baker Store,[7] at the door in front of a room set aside for women's clothing by the men's underwear section, Nur Baba and Nigâr talked quietly standing face-to-face.

Nur Baba said, "I was just about to miss the chance to see you. You went away from the carriage with such speed and entered this place, disappearing from sight so quickly. Thankfully, a voice inside me said that you would be here. Because two years ago, after chasing after you for sometime—again in Beyoğlu—this was the place that I came the closest to you."

Nigâr replied, "That's strange! It's the memory of the same day that unconsciously drove me here. I had no idea what I was going to do or where to go. I was about to return home."

"What a condition that would have left me in! There are days, weeks even, that I drag myself around here…" said Baba.

Nigâr interrupted, "Oh God, that fat man in front of the pile of clothes is looking at you so intensely. Be careful, is he someone you know?"

"No, my love, no one here knows me. It's only my clothes that catch everyone's attention."

Nigâr continued, "Actually, in this shop behind us all the girls know me, but there's no harm. Let's go there if you like, since there are a lot of customers coming and going here. The overfamiliar glances of these store workers are aggravating my nerves."

"You're so cautious, always in control of your will. As for me, at these moments I lose myself. I get so confused and distraught that I forget where I am and what I'm doing."

---

7 This department store was founded by George Baker, an English businessman who settled in Istanbul after the Crimean War (1856). Baker stores multiplied in years, but they remained focused in the Beyoğlu district. They offered an array of products ranging from ready-made garments and bedclothes to home accessories and furniture. Their customers were the bourgeoisie and elites of Istanbul: Behzat Üsdiken, "Baker Mağazaları," in *Dünden Bugüne İstanbul Ansiklopedisi*, vol. 1 (İstanbul: Ana Basım, 1993), 551–552; Reşad Ekrem Koçu, "Baker (George)," in *İstanbul Ansiklopedisi*, vol. 4 (İstanbul: İstanbul Ansiklopedisi ve Neşriyat Kollektif Şirketi, 1960), 1886–1887.

"Don't say that, Baba! Be sure that what I did just now is the greatest act of carelessness, even insanity, for a woman like me…"

"How good of you, madame, well done. I was joking, but speaking seriously, what will become of us? Mon petit chou? Apple of my eye?"

"I should ask you…or your master, that despotic old queen…"

"Don't go into that, for God's sake. You took everyone's word for it and really believed that she was something serious in my life. I swear that if you want…"

"Ey, continue."

"What need is there to explain?! How many times did I write, how many times did I say that I'm ready for anything? But you…"

"But me? Well, Master, let's imagine that I'm ready too…" she replied.

At this moment, one of the girls from the store approached them. Addressing Nigâr, she said:

"Let me give you a chair. You've been standing so long," she said.

The young woman said that they wouldn't be staying long, raised her eyes cautiously to Nur Baba and waited for his response to her earlier question; he thought a bit and then said:

"Tomorrow evening or in the day if the evening doesn't work, would you like to meet at Afife's house?"

"Who would Afife be?"

"How quickly you forgot! Alhotoz Afife, she lives in Sultantepe."

"Oh fine, fine."

She looked around as if she feared that her affirmative reply would be heard. Then she turned her shadowy eyes again to Nur Baba with a sweet sadness and laughed with her smile of myriad meanings, pulling the corner of her mouth upwards. Nur Baba asked:

"When should we expect you?"

"Tomorrow before noon, before noon."

The following day, Nigâr was at Alhotoz Afife's house before noon. Nur Baba had been waiting for her since morning and drinking the whole time to overcome the anxiety of the wait. It was as if he were a twenty-year-old and Nigâr were the first woman he had ever waited for. How many times did he say to Alhotoz Afife, with his voice trembling, "What if she doesn't come, what will we do? Tell me!" By the time Nigâr came into the room, Nur Baba couldn't muster the strength to get up. He was sitting beside the large tile-stove on top of a special cushion wearing the straw-colored summer silk robe that Nigâr liked so much. In front of him were a wine glass and a bottle:

"Nigâr, my child, forgive me. I can't get up," he said.

The niece of Madame Ziba walked toward him, laughing, and wanted to pay homage and kneel before him. But Nur Baba suddenly gathered all his strength, kneeled down on the floor and hugged the feet of the young woman who was preparing to kiss his knees:

"Bless these feet, bless them. Let me rub them on my face and my eyes," he said.

Nigâr was both surprised and happy from this enthusiastic greeting:

"For God's sake, Master, what are you doing? Please, I beg you," she said as she pulled away.

Then, with the swiftness of a horse, Nur Baba grabbed the young woman, who had still not taken off her overcoat, by the waist and squeezed her with a strength that felt like he was taking possession of her, such that Nigâr felt as if in one instant her complete being had mixed with his. Alhotoz Afife stood in the middle of the room watching this frantic encounter in utter shock, her eyes bulging. There was a beastly smile on her wrinkled, toothless, gnarled mouth. She muttered to herself:

"Whatever will happen, will happen today. It's clear."

Tottering, she silently made her way outside like a ghost wandering around the fire of a sorcerer.

10 The Woman with No Voice*

For perhaps the fifth time, Nigâr stopped at the window and yelled to Dervish Çinari, but somehow she couldn't make her voice heard.

Poor Dervish Çinari had truly aged: he was hard of hearing, his back was hunched, and his eyes had lost their sparkle. His utterly enigmatic face no longer expressed anything, and he continued the jobs that he used to do while singing songs and *nefes* in a gradually deepening silence.

For the sixth time, Nigâr looked out the window. Dervish Çinari was only thirty or forty steps from this window. Because the weather was tranquil and the season was winter, the tree branches that surrounded the lodge were bare. Nigâr saw him through the branches: he was busy sorting out the ripe from the unripe cabbages. Sir Safa's granddaughter was surprised by what the years had done to this man and said, "Poor Çinari can't hear," but she was not aware of what the years had done to her own voice.

For some time now, helpless Nigâr had been a woman with a raspy voice. Sometimes she attributed it to a chronic cold, other times to a nervous break-down, and was sure that one day her voice would clear up again. However, Nur Baba, who had neglected her for some time now, did not share her opinion, and thought that her body, like her voice, was in irreparable shape. Though this opinion about Nigâr was quite exaggerated, this man, who, as his age advanced, hated older women, was not completely wrong. No one could say that Nigâr was an old woman because she had just turned thirty-seven. But the life that she had entered for the last five or six years, those twenty-four-hour drinking sessions, the non-stop urges of *muhabbet*, and Nur Baba's tiring love had worn down this poor woman before her time. It made her almost unrecognizable and her voice hoarse, not due to the weight of the years, but rather the effects of her living conditions. Who could endure that many drinks and cigarettes, that much yelling, and so many sleepless nights?

One last time, Nigâr opened the window and yelled at Dervish Çinari with her raspy voice, and suddenly she collapsed on a cushion beside her, her face blue, with the exhaustion of a person who had lifted a heavy load, while her

---

* In the original version, this section is Supplement (Zeyil): Part I.

DOI: 10.4324/9781003381471-11

throat clogged up with coughing. For a week, Safa Efendi's granddaughter had been completely alone with Dervish Çinari in the lodge. Baba, Celile, and the lodge people had moved into the home of one of the female disciples in Kadıköy to spend the months of January, February, and March. Actually, they insisted that Nigâr come along too, but Madame Ziba's niece, despite everything, maintained her pride. She couldn't go on lengthy visits easily like the others, and, if she did, she felt uneasy deep inside and supposed that she had sunk to the level of Nuriye and Atiye. The thing she most feared was resembling these two old parasites. This was the Atiye who at one time brought Baba's letters to her, and Nuriye was the regular cup bearer. They were talked to when there was something for them to do; outside of this, their presence was seen as annoying, and sometimes they were completely ignored. The one whose face was corroded by old-fashioned make-up and the other whose nose was bulbous from alcohol could make a person feel nothing other than disgust and pity.

However, Nigâr's position in the lodge was no different from these women. They too had arrived young, fresh, and respected, and for a while they were held in high esteem and sat beside Baba during the *muhabbet*. Then, slowly, they began to lose all their respect and fell into this status. However, Nigâr still believed that she was respected, loved, and sought after. Even if the reality of the situation was not so, Safa Efendi's granddaughter could still adopt this lodge like her own home for the rest of her life. Because the lodge of Nur Baba, which was a building in ruins ready to collapse when she arrived as a guest, had become an impressive mansion, thanks to her and her money.[1] The entire lodge, down to the carpets in the *meydan* and every piece of furniture, was hers. Though—preserving her honor, good manners, and politeness—Nigâr never even thought of these things and placed her hopes in nothing besides Baba's *muhabbet*. The thing that had kept her in this lodge for six years was not this furniture and new roof that she knew came from her own wealth. It was only a look, a smile, or a word from the shaykh.

Wasn't it for this that she left everything? Her husband and children? Where was her mother? How many days did she mourn when her mother died because of her? How many hours did she cry after her children went to live with her husband in order not to see her again? Didn't she forget everything about her life the moment when Baba looked into her eyes and her entire being dazzled?

Yes, Sir Safa's granddaughter had forgotten everything. She remembered nothing pertaining to her past. It was as if she had lived here always, that she had been born and grew up here. Those who analyzed the poor woman's fate from a distance said that her fondness for alcohol had become a sickness.

---

1 Likewise, during the leadership of Ali Nutki Baba, the Çamlıca Lodge underwent a major renovation that transformed a decrepit structure into a mansion (*konak*): Maden, "Çamlıca," p. 225.

Alcohol? Nigâr now drank so much that she couldn't feel either relaxed or drunk. If she could only be drunk, if only she could appease that incessant need with five or ten glasses like she used to.

For a while, Nigâr became fast friends with Dervish Çinari, who said that he was addicted to the same substance in the past. Dervish Çinari had become like that manservant in her childhood from whose shoulders she never descended. Actually, for some time now, she had enjoyed talking with this half-crazed, half-enlightened man once in a while. However, in recent days, among all the people of the lodge, she spoke almost exclusively with him. Çinari quickly found cures for her troubles and also brought her medicine that gave her head sweet fantasies and calmed the everpresent tickling cough in her throat. Every time Dervish Çinari gave Nigâr some pills that looked like plant seeds collected from the ground, he never forgot to say, "Careful, don't let anyone see them! These are really hard to find." Following his advice, Nigâr either smoked these with tobacco or ground them and drank them in her coffee, so as not to show anyone. These medicines were the reason for her calling Çinari so insistently just now. For two days, she had been in a dreadful state without them and couldn't shake her addiction. Her appetite had disappeared, her nerves were a wreck, she was going crazy from boredom, and her cough had become so bad that she couldn't sleep at night. As for the nights...the nights that Nur Baba was far away, they were dark, terrifying, endless abysses.

Nigâr gave up on yelling out the window in vain, and decided to go to Çinari. He was busying himself among the cabbages in the garden. Sir Safa's granddaughter put on one of Baba's furs and went out to him. It was cold. Trembling, the poor woman wrapped herself in the thin fur and walked on the wet and muddy ground in flat woolen slippers. She approached Çinari and called out, "My friend, what's going on, you've lost yourself in your work again!"

The elderly dervish lifted his head and examined her with great care, as if he were seeing the woman standing above him for the first time; then he returned to his previous occupation.

"The good cabbage is gone. By God, these small ones are good for pickling..." he began to mumble.

"Well, just a minute ago my throat went hoarse yelling for you. I thought that you'd fallen asleep."

"I'd be lying if I said I hadn't; I lost myself a bit."

"In this cold! In this damp weather!"

"What do I care about hot or cold? Especially after swallowing a few of those..."

"Well, that's why I was calling you. Weren't you going to bring me some today?"

"I brought some but there aren't any left. I took them all."

"So now I go without any medicine!"

Dervish Çinari shrugged his shoulders. He didn't respond and Nigâr looked around with hopeless eyes. These eyes had too much kohl makeup, so much that you couldn't see the whites when she moved them. It was as if two pieces of coal were smoking secretly and emitting soot around them.

Nigâr, Nigâr, the white dove of just a few years ago! What happened to you, the gentle young woman that young Macid couldn't bring himself to look in the face? What transpired? What are these wrinkles around your eyes and on your forehead, these lines drooping the corners of your mouth? Your hair is so unkempt, such a tangled mess. Don't you ever brush it anymore? And what has happened to the color, beautiful Nigâr? You dyed it so awfully, in light and dark colors! You had hair as soft as silk! Now there's no difference between it and a horse's mane that has been neglected. What is happening? A strange shrinking is occurring to your lips. That charming dimple, that used to pull up one corner of those lips, now pulls your mouth crooked to the side, like the trace of an old wound. Are you in pain? Why do you contract your lips like this? Why do you distort your face like that? Poor woman, in the middle of this bare, damp winter scene, you're such a sad sight to behold!

Nigâr suddenly squatted beside Çinari as if a knot had been untied in her knees. She was dragging the fur wrapped around her in the mud. Dervish Çinari turned his head and looked again at the woman:

"Be careful, you're getting Baba's fur dirty," he said.

"Yes," she said. "Today I'm depressed, my friend. Should I get up and go down to Kadıköy?"

Dervish Çinari shrugged his shoulders in a way that conveyed the meaning "Do whatever you want." He stood up, took the cabbage in his arms, and walked slowly toward the lodge without saying a word to Nigâr. The young woman stayed for a long while in the middle of the vegetable garden. Under the leafless trees, the wintery meadow transmitted incredible melancholia to her soul. It was so depressing that not even the graveyard off to the left looked more sorrowful. Just as Nigâr turned her head and looked in that direction, with the feeling of someone after long sleeplessness imagining their bed, she thought, "When I die, I'll sleep here." She got up slowly and went toward the rows of stone that appeared whiter than necessary in the pale winter light. Often, in moments when she didn't know what to do with her depression and boredom, like today, Nigâr strolled around this small graveyard. She found a thousand things to keep her busy. Sometimes, she straightened a tombstone that was falling over, tried to cover an eroding pit with earth, picked out aggressive weeds that grew in inappropriate places, and even though she knew them by heart, she read the inscriptions every time she saw them. A large portion of these inscriptions were from Nur Baba's writings, some of them verse, some of them prose. But in all of them was something that reminded one of Nur Baba's style, his voice, his accent, and his speech. Here was the tomb of a woman by the name of Madame Perestev who, before Nigâr took initiation, had thrown herself out of a window of the lodge after one of Baba's cruel moments; she remained in the house paralyzed for a long time and her will stipulated that she must be buried here. Actually, Madame Ziba's niece had seen this woman in her last days and had even liked her more than the others she met. What tender, sweet, familiar eyes she had!

This victim of *muhabbet*, who hadn't been heard from in years, had begun to send Nur Baba news every day, and her laments had become unceasing. Finally, the prosperous woman took her last breath with her hand in Baba's. That's why the epitaph that Nur Baba composed was a long, burning elegy.

Nigâr read this dirge again for perhaps the hundreth time. Actually, this dirge was no masterpiece. The meter and rhyme had mistakes from beginning to end. But for Sir Safa's granddaughter, this was one of the most beautiful pieces of Turkish literature. As she recited it, she lost herself and found, especially in these lines, a sublimity whose secret was beyond comprehension:

> *Pesterev is a guest in the garden of hearts*
> *The only beloved among the lovers*
> *Why did she come and pass by without stopping?*
> *Blessed is the one who departs for good, not those who stay*
> *But woe, what state is death*
> *Not a word comes from those who go, so of course we fear it*

After wandering among the many tombstones large and small, Nigâr stopped in front Alhotoz Afife's grave. One night three years ago, this woman died suddenly during the Ceremony of Union. Madame Ziba's niece couldn't bear to sit beside her in the early days but, over time, had become so used to her that she wouldn't leave her side even for a day. Alhotoz Afife had served Sir Safa's granddaughter's every need in the first period of her relations with Nur Baba. Nigâr had passed her first night alone with Baba, far from everyone—and that was a night of love—in Afife's house in Üsküdar. Later, it was revived again many times in the same place and, thanks to Afife, gossip and many rumors were prevented from spreading. Nur Baba engraved these words on this woman's tombstone:

> *The loyal servant of the graceful Path, Mother Afife, is buried here. This loving soul expired in this honored lodge. Ali, Hak, Hu!*

Right beside Alhotoz Afife lay Nakip Pasha's wife. This soul was the elderly woman whose mansion in Üsküdar was the winter residence of Nur Baba year after year. Surrounded by an iron railing, her tomb was made of stunning marble and had a respectful elegy engraved on it. Nigâr didn't dwell in front of it for long. A bit further back, she reached Colonel Hamdi's grave. Poor Hamdi! Of the men who attended the lodge regularly, she liked him the most. He carried such refined sentiments under his simple, coarse appearance!

He was so gracious and understanding and had such bizarre mannerisms and witty things to say. Nigâr saw the real Bektashi, in every sense, in this man. Not once did the late Hamdi get sad, angry, or worried about something related to him. The saying, *No matter what they do to him, he is thankful, no matter what they do to him, he is merry,* guided his behavior.[2] He was subject to all kinds of insults in the lodge, but he didn't say a thing, and never held a grudge against anyone. Sometimes his gentleness and peaceful nature reached a degree to which they were annoying. With her eyes filled with tears, Nigâr remembered how, a few times, she had grabbed him by the shoulders and yelled, "Hamdi, Hamdi, say something, do something! For God's sake!" Laughing, he would say, "*Eyvallah, eyvallah,* my sister, I don't have a problem with anyone! *Eyvallah!*"

Eyvallah![3] Isn't this the underlying philosophy of Bektashism? Doesn't it all stem from what this word expresses? Laying your hand over your heart, bowing your head, leaving yourself to the spiritual pleasure of humility and modesty; to say "*Eyvallah! Eyvallah!*" to insult, to cruelty, to oppression, to offense and enemies! What else besides realizing this lofty goal could be the secret of this order? Outside this spiritual state, Nigâr found all other conditions destructive, unfortunate, and unbearable. What is all that struggling over self-love and concern for dignity and honor? Who are those misfortunate, unlucky souls who spend their whole lives agitated over their pride? Instead of loving, they want to be loved. They become jealous, they yell, they call out, and they believe in useless things like conquering and being conquered.

Nigâr said to herself, "To love, always to love! To love the one in front of us without expecting anything, to always give of ourselves, not to be sorry, not to regret, but to love, to love always!"

Those who had not learned this secret were surprised at Nigâr's patience. While Nur Baba became drinking partners with others in front of her, they could not understand how she quietly observed such a scene, and, therefore, they all concluded that Nigâr was callous and stupid. Madame Ziba was the ringleader of those who judged the situation as such. Madame Ziba had completely withdrawn from the world of *muhabbet* and, though she had devoted herself to matters like poker and commerce, from a distance she still concerned herself with the affairs of the lodge, her heart's first home. Of Nigâr, she used to say:

---

2 Some sources attribute this saying to the poet Fuzûlî. Fuzûlî, or Muhammad b. Sulayman (d. 1556), was an important poet, who composed in Arabic, Persian, and Turkish. He is remembered in Turkey for his Turkish-language verse, particularly his *Divan, Leyla ve Mecnun,* and *Beng ü bade,* a poem dedicated to the Safavid Shah Ismail that compares opium and wine, ultimately, declaring wine to be superior. Among Bektashis, he is revered because of his work "Hadîkatü's-Süedâ" in the genre *maktel-i Hüseyin* about the events of Karbala and the martyrdom of Husayn.

3 The word conveys a sense of gratefulness and acceptance. In colloquial speech, it can mean "alright" or "thanks," but it carries a deeper connotation of accepting everything as a means of embracing God's will and the fullness of reality.

"I said it for a long time. She has a heart like a stone and a scattered mind. She's one of the insane ones."

As Nigâr heard this, she laughed with that enigmatic style that pulled up one corner of her mouth and was always in a state of contraction in recent times:

"Yes, I'm insane!" she burst out. As she said this, she remembered that verse in the first Bektashi hymn she ever heard:

We are meticulous and have a clear head but
We're the fools of Pir Sultan Balım

How does it happen that those who, for years, take pride in being a Bektashi become so blind and muddled not to see the path described by these two lines? Nigâr was an experienced, mature soul that had attained all the secrets of the spiritual life. So much so that she felt infinite pleasure even when she burned with anger inside, and so she stroked, warmed, and fed the pains that continually clawed at her chest. How many times did Macid, one of her relatives, send news and try to rescue her from the pit she was in? How many times did he say, "Nigâr, I'm still in the place where you left me. I'm alone and waiting for you." But Nigâr understood that she couldn't find joy or peace in anything except this pain and this curse, and so she stayed where she was.

"To love, to love always, despite insults, rejection, oppression, wounding words and curse, denials, and ridicule—to love," she would say.

Nigâr, your eyes smoke deep inside like embers of coal, you are certainly the sister of Husayn or the wife of Hallaj-i Mansur![4] Roses bloom in the ground where you bleed and the air that blows around your ashes smells of ambergris. You've become tipsy by these scents and roses. Oh, you, eternally intoxicated by the primordial gathering of souls, the Feast of "Am I Not?".[5]

4 Husayn was the grandson of the Prophet Muhammad and the son of the prophet's daughter Fatima and the prophet's cousin Ali. Husayn died at Karbala in the year 680 CE at the hands of an Umayyad army. His sister Zainab mourned his death publicly and became integral to rituals and narrative of commemorating Husayn and his family's death during Ashura, the first ten days of the month of Muharram in the Hijri calendar. Hallaj, Al-Husayn b. Mansur al-Hallaj (d. 922) was a Sufi who was executed in Baghdad on charges that he claimed that the required Islamic pilgrimage to the Kaba in Mecca could be substituted with a visit to a replica of the Kaba that he had built in his yard. A popular legend holds that Hallaj uttered, in a state of spiritual merger with God, *I am the Truth* and was "executed as a Sufi by the political establishment because he had attempted to reveal the shocking truth at the heart of Sufi thought and practice to those who could not have possibly understood it." Karamustafa, *Sufism: The Formative Period*, 25–26. His utterance *I am the Truth—Enelhak*—made Hallaj revered by Bektashis and is widely used in Bektashi poetry.

5 The term *bezm-i elest* (Feast of "Am I Not?") refers to a conversation between God and the children of Adam in Qur'an 7: 172 in which God asks: "Am I not your Lord?" They said, "Yes, we testify." In Turkish Sufi literature, the term refers to the covenant between God and humankind established in a gathering of souls before they enter their bodies at which love and awareness of God began. The "wine" consumed at this primordial feast invokes the

Nigâr felt she was getting cold, even wearing Baba's fur. The sky had become dark, and now she couldn't distinguish any of the inscriptions. Slowly, she returned to the lodge. But the lodge was in darkness. She screamed from the entrance:

"Çinari, Çinari!"

From the kitchen all the way in the back of the lodge, the dishes and pots the old dervish pulled out were making noise. Beating the walls with her hand, Nigâr advanced step by step and hollered again with her completely hoarse voice in the coolness of the evening:

"Çinari, Çinari!"

The kitchen door slowly opened, letting out dusty, muddled light and Dervish Çinari held out a large lamp into the courtyard:

"It wouldn't hurt to have a bite to eat. What do you say Nigâr?" he said.

"intoxication of ecstasy which comes with any unusual glmpse of Absolute Beauty" and, hence, the term "Elest" often appears in Sufi poetry, e.g.:

From eternity we are intoxicated with the wine of Unity.
We are of those who have tasted the cup of Elest

Birge, *Bektashi Order*, 112–113.

11 That World, Yet Again*

Today is Nevruz.[1] Nur Baba went up to the lodge with the entire group. Since yesterday, inside the lodge they had been working feverishy making exhaustive preparations, from the kitchen to the bedrooms. Despite feeling uncomfortable, even Nigâr participated. She ironed all the clean towels, bed sheets, and pillowcases because Celile had become so weak that she was not fit for work anymore. In every movement, a part of the poor woman's body hurt, and her exhaustion ended either in aching kidneys or the swelling of the varicose veins in her legs.

Since morning, Nur Baba had been occupied only with greeting the guests and disciples that flowed in through the doors of the lodge. Though, traditionally, Nevruz is celebrated in the garden, this time they all gathered around an enormous oven in a small room because the weather was too cold. Despite this, the women wore pink and white robes in honor of Nevruz and the men put seasonal flowers in their collars. Nur Baba's stiff body was also in soft, thin fabric, and his beard smelled of various fragrances. On his face that no line had spoiled for the last six years, the beard looked more black and magnificent than ever. A certain gravitas that exuded dignity had descended upon him. He didn't laugh too much, say too much, or fall into excessively friendly behavior as he used to. There was a shadow of sweet sadness in his eyes.

The disciples interpreted his demeanor as being a manifestation of his new love. Everyone believed that, this time, Nur Baba had been fatally ensnared because, for the last six months, a newly emerging beauty that never left his side in *muhabbet* had wrapped up the *pir*, who was well over forty-five, in a passion that surrounded him on all sides like a spell. At this moment, this girl named Süheyla was filling Nur Baba's glass from a small, pink decanter and no one present, man or woman, could stop themselves from looking at least once, even obliquely, at her ivory-colored, delicate, smooth wrists. Her elegant neck that extended like music from the open collar of her rose-colored

---

* In the original version, this section is Supplement (Zeyil): Part II.

1 Nevruz, the Persian New Year festival, is celebrated at the spring equinox.

DOI: 10.4324/9781003381471-12

crepe dress reminded one of the necks of swans that moved in the water as it turned pink with the last rays of the sun. She was one of those girls who, while looking at her face even in the bleakest times, a person feels a sweet freshness and wonderful vitality in the heart, as if they had arrived at the waterfront on a summer day. Doesn't every fresh maiden have this gleaming clarity of water? And isn't every virgin playful and traitorous like water? Even when their bodies, which cannot even be naked for themselves, strip in front of us from head to toe, they still remain covered. They obtain all their strength from the secret they carry. And because they have never tried to engage the power of love, their opposition to a lover is powerful. Does marble have the same hardness of a young woman's heart?

One should ask Nur Baba. Nur Baba, who knew how to melt the hardest, toughest heart in an instant, now looked like a novice child beside Süheyla. He didn't know how to win her over. Now and then he asked:

"Girl, where is your heart?"

Süheyla laughed and replied:

"I don't have a heart."

As she drank, her sobriety increased, and when Nur Baba touched her, her body became even stiffer.

"Leave me alone, I'm still not ready," she said and took refuge in Celile's embrace. One time she put her arms around Nigâr's neck. The poor woman didn't know what to do and stayed put. Nur Baba tried in vain to separate the two bodies from one another. The young girl was practically glued to Nigâr. During this contact, Nur Baba's old love Nigâr felt that no part of the young girl's body was trembling. Even her heart beat steadily, not slower or faster than usual, and Nigâr said to herself, "What a shame. She doesn't love, doesn't feel anything. His hands touch her and her body is still like a stone!" And she thought that a body that remained this calm against the wild assaults of love would have no importance, no value in the eyes of those who understood the ways of the heart, no matter how lively the body, no matter how fresh and beautiful. Isn't it also in part because of this that Nigâr had never thought to be jealous of Nur Baba? According to her, Nur Baba's addiction to her was nothing but a passing desire. She waited saying that he would drop Süheyla today or tomorrow. But this Nevruz, just as everyone began to gather together, drink sherbet, eat candies, and pass the pot of spiced taffy from hand to hand, Nur Baba spoke with that stage voice particular to him:

"Dear souls, I have some good news for you. Next week, my wedding with Süheyla will take place."

As soon as he said this, poor Nigâr, who was already sick and fatigued, suddenly felt her heart stop and short of breath. Süheyla looked straight ahead with a composed, serious coolness that also bespoke a bit of sadness. Celile got up, paid homage to Baba, and kissed the young girl's forehead. All together, the disciples shouted, "Congratulations, congratulations!" Nigâr didn't know what happened after that. She felt dizzy and dull, like a heavy

blow had been delivered to her head. Nur Baba looked at her from the corner
of his eye:

"Nigâr, what's wrong?"

The young woman convulsed as if waking from a nightmare. The voice
from the man across from her seemed to come from so far away:

"Who, me?" she asked.

Everyone started to laugh. To change the subject, Nur Baba mumbled a
line from Fuzûlî:

"If you are you, then who am I, my love?"

And he turned to the *oud*-player Niyazi:

"Come on, move a bit!" he said.

Niyazi began an improvisation from the musical mode *Acem Aşiran.*[2]
Süheyla served as the cupbearer. Nigâr didn't know what happened afterward.
Now all the sounds of the gathering, all the instruments, were like the horrible
cries of the apocalypse in her brain. She saw everything happening before her
through a fog: Nur Baba's glances, the movements of his mouth, Süheyla's
studiously proper comportment, the *oud*-player Niyazi's hand fluttering over
the strings, Celile bending and straightening up, Nesimi rocking from side to
side with the music. They gave her *rakı*, she drank it. They passed her the pot
of taffy, she ate it. But for her, the taste of what she ate and drank was like the
taste of eating or drinking something in a dream; its true nature had unclear
qualities and, also as if in a dream, she couldn't control her actions with her
own will.

A bit later, Nur Baba called out again:

"Nigâr, Nigâr."

He signaled for her to come to his side; Nigâr got up and went. She squeezed
in between Nur Baba and Celile. The master of *muhabbet* took her hands in
his and asked in a soft voice:

"What's wrong, my dear? What's wrong?"

Madame Ziba's niece looked with astonishment at the man asking her this
absurd question. She could no longer recognize him. Who is this man? *Who is
this man*? Where, how, and why had he got mixed up in her life? What did this
black beard and pale face represent? In an instant, all the faces that she had
left behind rushed through her mind. Despite all the time and distance, they
appeared closer to her than this man.

Arrive, arrive, dear faces of the past! Nigâr lost her way in an endless desert.
The poor thing, she had been walking for years and whatever there was in her
pouch to eat and drink was now finished. She was face to face with a sphinx
squatting at the edge of an empty pit, and the sphinx's eyes were emptier and
drier than the pit.

A powerful shiver overtook her body. Nur Baba said:

"You're sick, you should definitely go to bed."

---

2 *Acem Aşiran* is a musical mode in Ottoman classical music.

Forget about walking, Nigâr could not even stand. Through chattering teeth, she said:

"Leave me! Let me curl up and lie down here awhile!" collapsing like bundle unraveling on the edge of Nur Baba's rug. The guide took off his robe, covered the woman, and gently stroked her back for a while. All of wretched Nigâr's limbs were trembling. Celile said:

"She can't sleep here. Master, she should definitely go to bed!"

"God damn it, leave me in peace!" groaned Nigâr.

Nur Baba began to read his new composition, a poem called "Nevruziye," to encourage the *muhabbet* that had been interrupted by this event. Like all his other compositions, it lacked meter and rhyme. But from the first line, those at the gathering began to listen with reverence. Even Nesimi, who had been drinking for quite some time with Muallim Nâci and his disciple, opened his eyes now and then making artificial gestures that expressed attention and concern.[3] For instance, verses like:

> The nightingale said to the rose, Come rose
> The rose said to the nightingale, I won't

Met with cries like:

"*Aman, aman,* what masterful artistry!"

Continually raising his hands in the air, Necati, who had at one time published many verses in a periodical that the poet Andelib published, shouted out:[4]

"Read it again, Master, for the love of God, once more!"

With her eyes closed, Celile swayed left and right, and the oudist Niyazi turned to those beside him and said in a voice that Nur Baba could hear:

"Let's put this to music right away!"

Leaning her head on the shaykh's shoulder, Süheyla followed the lines he was reading with furtive glances. However, Nur Baba was the one who was enraptured. While he recited, he took advantage of the young girl's body pressed against him, letting his empty hand wander around her waist. Nigâr slowly stuck her head out from under the covers, and when her eyes encountered this sincere embrace between Süheyla and Nur Baba, she immediately covered her face again. She said to herself, "If only I could get up and leave!" At that moment, she would have liked above anything to get in bed, lie face down, and bawl her eyes out. When the time had come that

---

3 Muallim Nâci (1849–93) was a poet, author, translator, literary critic, and educator. He authored a wide range of works in different genres and on different subjects including popular history and religion. In 1891, Sultan Abdülhamid II tasked him with writing on Ottoman history and granted him a salary and official rank for this purpose. He was buried in the graveyard of Sultan Mahmud II's mausoleum on the Divanyolu in Istanbul: *TDV*, "Muallim Nâci."

4 Another reference to the poet/editor "Andelib" Mehmet Faik Esat of *rakı* drinking fame. He served as the editor of several journals, including *Hazine-i Fünun, Mektep,* and *İrtika*: Gisela Procházka-Eisl, "Andelib, Mehmet Esat," in: *Encyclopaedia of Islam, Volume Three.*

Nevruz was over, Nur Baba folded the paper in his hand in four with great care and placed it in a large bound folder and then turned to Süheyla and sang Nedim's lines:[5]

Shall I be the cupbearer when the feast begins, my love,
instead of you with crystal arms reminiscent of silver?

He motioned with his eyes to the glass he was finishing.

Süheyla filled it and held it out for him, but Nur Baba didn't take the wineglass from her hand. He grabbed her wrist and brought the glass to his lips with the cupbearer's fingers, just like an ecstatic Rifai dervish puts fire in his mouth, and tasted the pleasure of *rakı* and the kiss together.[6] The young girl pulled away, her body trembling and shaking, and moved coquettishly as she passed out *rakı* to everyone with the same coyness and haughtiness.

Towards evening, new guests began to arrive alone and in pairs. Among them were initiated and uninitiated attendees, and most of them—like Sister Celile's nieces—were from the lodge group. Sensing the growing crowd, Nigâr showed her desire to go and sleep.

On one side, Nur Baba was talking with those arriving and on the other, he said to his old love:

"Let me take you, child, let me take you. Let me put you in bed and cover you. The others are no good."

A bit later, Nigâr was in a position that could be said to be in Nur Baba's lap. Wrapped around each other, they got up and left.

Süheyla bit her lip in rage. However, if she had followed them, she would have realized that this rage was misplaced, for Nur Baba had only shown this compassion in front of everyone present in order to demonstrate the gratitude he owed to Nigâr. So as soon as they entered the courtyard, he only went to

---

5 Nedim (d. 1730), born in Istanbul, was an Ottoman poet and teacher who became well-known for a style of *divan* poetry, which, thereafter, came to be known by his name.

6 "Rifai" refers to the Sufi lineage descended from Ahmad al-Rifaʿi (d. 1182), a shaykh based in lower Iraq. In the Ottoman realm, the Rifai became well-known for performing acts of self-mortification, such as piercing the limbs and mouth with skewers and swallowing fire. Western observers and scholars often referred to them as "howling" ecstatic dervishes, contrasting them with the more measured and dignified "whirling" Mevlevis. "The howling [Rifai] and whirling [Mevlevi] dervishes deserve particular attention. These are the two most curious Sufi sects, both in terms of the strangeness of their exercises, and the insight they offer into a better understanding of the dervish lodge institution in Islam. As their names indicate, one group howls, as the other waltzes": "Derviches tourneurs," *Magasin Pittoresque*, 1839, p. 71 from *The Istanbul Research Institute Blog* < https://blog.iae.org.tr/en/exhibitions/the-performance-of-dervishes> For a description of travelers' reactions to these ceremonies, see Reinhold Schiffer, *Oriental Panorama: British Travellers in 19th Century Turkey* (Amsterdam: Rodopi, 1999), 200–203.

the trouble of holding out his arm for the sick woman, and as they came to the bedroom door, he practically grabbed her by the shoulder and threw her into the room. But Nigâr didn't let go of his arm; suddenly, she spoke with a commanding and authoritative voice:

"You're not leaving, you're not leaving. You're staying with me!"

In these words there was such a violent decisiveness, that with a submissiveness he felt for the first time in his life, Nur Baba followed the woman quietly and obediently. Nigâr closed the door, turned the key twice, and put it in her pocket. After this, the shaykh became despondent:

"How can this happen, Nigâr? They're waiting for me downstairs…"

Without responding, Nigâr pulled him toward her. Both of them fell on the wide cushion. The room was dark.

Nur Baba said, "Let me turn on the light, at least."

Nigâr wanted to stay in the dark. And she was saying:

"Tonight I'm afraid of sound, movement and light. Shut up, sit beside me, don't talk, don't move. And don't touch me! Tonight I'm a different creature. I'm an astounding creature from far away that has seen things you've never seen and heard things you've never heard. Who are you? I don't know. If you speak, I won't understand your language, but I want you beside me because I'm scared of being alone. Together with the brightness of all the things I know, the things I learned, I'm scared of being alone face to face with this terrifying emptiness inside my head. Ah, I've never felt as lonely as tonight. For months, you and everyone else have been in Kadıköy, and I've been all alone here with Dervish Çinari. But I don't know, I don't remember if I've ever been so frightened before by loneliness. What should I do? Where can I go that I won't feel this loneliness? I'll stay side by side, head to head, with those who know the things I know. Without me saying anything, they can explain, without them saying anything, I can explain."

Nur Baba said:

"My dear, you're sick. You have a fever! You're raving; lie down and I'm going to send Nuriye up to you. If you want, Celile will come up and look after you."

Seeing that she didn't reply, he assumed that she was content. He reached out his hand toward the pocket where the key was. The woman grabbed the hand moving over her and squeezed it so hard that Nur Baba almost screamed. Nigâr said:

"Do you see? I'm not the weak, puny, gentle, unopposing Nigâr. I too have new powers. For how long? I don't know, I don't know…neither you nor I can say. However these powers, these are the powers that you have given me. Don't you know? I became like this in your hands."

With eyes that could be seen even in the dark, she looked into Nur Baba's eyes. Her already hoarse voice worsened as she spoke, turning into something like a drunk's growl.

Nur Baba wanted to get up and leave again and, this time, used the technique of fooling Nigâr by stroking her. But the young woman pushed back the hands that came toward her in the darkness:

"Didn't I say not to touch me? You're outrageous," she said. "I know this body is yours. You created it and you ruined it. Before running into you, it was young, fresh, and vital. After running into you, under your hands, between your arms, it lost all its youth, all its vitality. But before, it had no value. It was a foolish, callous, unfeeling body that didn't know you. Now every part of it knows something, feels something. It remembers, it thinks. If I go blind one day, I'll be able to see you with the tips of my fingers. Now my meat, my flesh are experience, knowledge, and mind, from head to toe. But Nur Baba, what a shame that it now has no value whatsoever in your view. Is this what you cultivated me for?"

Here Nigâr's voice broke up in hiccups. Nur Baba viewed this crying as the beginning of peace and acted as if he were crying in order to increase the sick woman's tears. He covered his face with his hands.

Right at this moment, someone knocked on the door. Celile's voice came from outside:

"Master, Recep Pasha's family came; the *meydan* is overflowing with people. I don't know what to say. It's a shame, they're all waiting for you..." she said.

Without speaking, Nigâr handed Nur Baba the key. With the look of a man interrupted while grieving, he stayed where he was with the key in his hand. Then he leaned over to the woman laying face-down on the bed weeping:

"How can I leave you in this state? There's no way, no way!" he said.

Nigâr pushed Nur Baba's head with the back of her hand and, with a voice hard to understand, said:

"Oh, you can go now. What's the difference if you stay here or there? It's all the same. Forgive me, I didn't know what I was doing. Forgive..."

And Nur Baba slowly slipped out of the room.

12 The Beloved Asked for the Soul*

After Nur Baba married Süheyla, Nigâr's state of mind became utterly enigmatic. She almost never came out of her room, she didn't talk with anyone in the lodge, and she always seemed to be immersed in deep thought. The crooked smile that used to be one of the most charming and attractive features of her face was now a grimace that pulled her drooping mouth to the side like the scar of a knife wound, and aside from the touching meaning this grimace conveyed, it expressed nothing else. Now and then, when Nur Baba found her alone, he would say:

"Nigâr, Nigâr...What happened to you? You're breaking my heart!"

Her eyes that understood nothing looked at Nur Baba's face, and then her head bowed forward and she was silent. Forget about attending the ceremonies and *muhabbet*, she didn't even come down for meals, even when there was no one in the lodge. Dervish Çinari brought first her *rakı* and then her food on a tray. Nigâr only talked with Dervish Çinari, and Dervish Çinari seemed human only in Nigâr's presence. This strange creature, whose beard had not seen a comb nor his hair scissors in years, wandered around outside Nigâr's room like a bogey man, reminiscent of prehistoric times. Nevertheless, the reasons for the bond between Nigâr and Dervish Çinari did not merely consist of the two being united in the same vile habit.

At first, the close friendship between this woman and man had been motivated by their shared addiction. Both of them had a fondness for hashish and opium, but, later, this bond became a completely spiritual relationship, like the affection between a dog and his master. Dervish Çinari knew what the young woman would say before she opened her mouth and Nigâr understood what he wanted from his glances. By these means, Dervish Çinari knew how much suffering Nigâr experienced, and Nigâr felt that he understood her pain.

---

* In the original, this section is Supplement (Zeyil): III. The title of this chapter "*Câni cânân dilemiş*" comes from a couplet by the poet Fuzûlî:

> O heart, the beloved asked for the soul, it is inappropriate not to give it / Why should we quarrel as it belongs neither to you nor to me
> (*Câni cânân dilemiş vermemek olmaz ey dil / Ne nizâ eyleyelim ol ne senindir ne benim*)

DOI: 10.4324/9781003381471-13

It was only in this feeling that Nigâr found something like comfort in her difficult solitude, and this feeling was the only thing that made her torment bearable. The heart of a person is, on the one hand, an insignificant child's toy, and on the other, an awe-inspiring precipice. Sometimes there is no joy, no pleasure, no exhiliration capable of cheering us up in times of major crisis. Other times, at the same level of crisis, something insignificant—a word, a look, a motion, a smile—can, even if it doesn't save us, help our patience and forbearance.

Since the day she donated all her wealth to Nur Baba, this addicted woman—who forgot her husband, mother, and children, who couldn't breathe for a moment outside of Nur Baba's world—wasn't disgusted, shocked, or hesitant when she accepted spiritual guidance said to be love and compassion, from this dubious creature, and in him, she found the faces and souls that formed the pure sweet memories of her childhood; the faces and souls of her nanny and manservant of her youth. Actually, in this house that increasingly estranged her and whose pleasant attributes were progressively diminishing, it was only this crazy Dervish Çinari that was concerned with the comfort of her body and peace of her heart as much as he was occupied with her food, drink, and clothing.

One day, he came to her side in an even more mysterious manner than usual, holding out a small envelope that he pulled out of his pocket. He said:

"Today in Kadıköy I ran into a gentleman, one of your relatives, who was he, what was his name? Wait, yes. You took initiation together."

Nigâr's heart skipped and her voice broke up.

"Macid? Was it Macid?" she asked.

Dervish Çinari nodded his head.

"God bless you! Yes, him! I passed by without recognizing him, you know, and he grabbed me by the arm. 'Where are you headed like that, not saying hello?' he asked. Then he immediately asked about you. When he said your name, I understood. Now and then he was asking, 'Is she well? Tell me the truth. How is she?' By the truth of the master, I told him. He thought and thought, and then said, 'If I write something down and give it you, will you take it and deliver it to her?' he asked. '*Eyvallah!*' I said. We entered a shop and he asked for a pen, a sheet of paper, and an envelope. He wrote this quickly, sealed it, and gave it to me."

After saying this, he looked around foolishly. Stunned and wretched, Nigâr held the envelope in her hand, and it seemed like she couldn't find the courage to open and read it.

"Open it, *yahu*! Maybe it's good news," Çinari said.

Nigâr opened it. This was the content of the letter:

It's been a week since I returned from Europe. As soon as I came, my first priority was going to be to see you. Somehow it hasn't been easy to do. I couldn't come to the place where you are. I thought that if I sent a letter it might not reach you. I called Aunt Ziba and heard that she's living a completely different life now. One even stranger than her previous one…

Forget about your name, she seemed to have forgotten even Nur Baba's name. A chance encounter that I didn't expect gave me the opportunity to write you these lines. I'm not sure if this is the best of all opportunities as I don't have much confidence in that crazy dervish. In any case, I definitely need to see you. Where? When? Inform me at this address as soon as possible: Nişantaşı Çubukçuyan Apartments, #8. If you wish, come straight there yourself. I live alone. I'm home every day until noon. For now, I kiss your hand.

The next day, Nigâr went to Macid's house. This was the first time she had gone out into the city in the last two years. How did she take the ferry from Üsküdar? How did she get from the ferry to the bridge? These steps each require separate description.

Nigâr took all these steps in a flash like movements in a dream. When she went up the stairwell at Çubukçuyan Apartments and entered Macid's flat, her feet no longer felt the ground and her eyes clouded up. A servant took her to a room, and two minutes later she saw Macid walking toward her from the doorway and fainted.

When she opened her eyes again, she found Macid seated beside her, rubbing strongly scented ointments on her hands, wrists, and temples. She looked at his face in shock; Macid was no less pale than Nigâr and his chin trembled unusually, preventing him from speaking.

Nigâr said:

"I scared you. It's nothing, it's nothing. Oh, I just wore myself out. Imagine, a woman that hasn't got out for two years suddenly takes a car, a ferry, another car, encounters the noise, the tumult, then the apartment stairs. All at once, in a dash."

Macid still didn't say anything and was looking carefully at Nigâr's face. Nigâr said:

"Did you bring some news about my children? You saw them, didn't you?"

The young man remained quiet. This time Nigâr became silent too and looked straight ahead. How long did this silence last? One minute? One hour? An entire day? Neither this faint woman nor this pale, trembling man could say because they were both in a gust of grief that blew away their voices and their words. And what need was there to talk? Didn't Nigâr's clothes, face, and condition clearly explain, page by page, to the young man the horrific ordeal that she had been through? What could she say that would explain the situation as clearly as her tired, exhausted eyes with badly applied make-up and the neglected hands and hair? Macid had known all her secrets the moment he entered the door and saw her. Why was his jaw shaking? Why had his face turned yellow? What could it be attributed to other than the shock of suddenly seeing, all at once, the scene behind the curtain that covered Nigâr, the six-year-long catastrophe of her life? Those who remember how concerned and bound Macid had been to Nigâr at one time would attribute his devastation to the inflamation of an old wound. But at this moment, the young man felt nothing but a deep and infinite pity in his heart for Nigâr. With the courage this acute weakness had given him, the young man quickly collected himself and spoke with a commanding, authoritative voice:

"Nigâr Abla," he said. "You're going to stay here. Let me send someone to bring your things, and when your children return to Istanbul, they will find you here in my house. Right here!"

This effect of this sudden and unexpected offer on Nigâr was stunning. She was completely thrown aback and asked, stammering:

"How?"

Macid had assumed that she would accept this offer with great joy. The young woman's response "How?" with a melancholy face, was completely contrary to his expectation and gave him a painful shock.

"What do you mean 'how'? Nigâr Abla, I know that you need someone to rescue you. I know how indecisive you are. Some dark impulses dragged you anywhere they wished against your will and you fell into an abyss. But you didn't make the smallest effort to save yourself, nor did you take the trouble to call out 'Come and save me' to those around you. I know you, Nigâr Abla; that's why, this time I'll deal with all the tiring business and you won't be bothered with a thing..."

Nigâr cut off the young man again:

"How?" she asked, hanging her head dejectedly.

Macid became serious and definitive:

"Like I just said; we'll send someone now to go and bring your things. There are six rooms here; you'll take two of them. In two or three months, your children will return. At that time, I'll make do with one room. I'll leave the whole apartment to you. Your daughter grew up; she's a young lady, did you know? She's now exactly thirteen. When we're alone, we always talk about you. She asked me, 'Do I look like my mother?' 'You're just like her,' I said. Her eyes glowed. Then they saddened and she asked, 'Do you know whose fault it was? Dad's or hers?' And I laughed and said, 'Oh, look at this whippersnapper putting her parents on trial!'"

Macid examined Nigâr's face as he explained this. He perceived no sign of grief other than this look of deep immersion on her face. The young man continued:

"And your son, what a rascal he is! He's rambunctious. I guess either he or we will have a handful of trouble in this apartment! One day..."

Nigâr interrupted Macid again:

"I should definitely go and pick up my things myself," she said.

At this point, Macid didn't recognize Nigâr Abla at all. He suddenly felt that her voice, expression, face, hair color, and clothes weren't the only things that had changed; at the same time, her gentle, pure heart had become coarse like her clothes, and old, unraveled, and prickly like her voice. Poor Macid couldn't tell if he should be angry or empathetic with the situation:

"Why do you think that's necessary?" he asked.

With an air of certainty, Nigâr replied:

"I don't want to offend anyone! It's true that I have no obligation to stay there forever. But we definitely have to make this decision together with him. Despite everything, you know that he is my spiritual master. I submitted myself to him. Without his permission..."

She couldn't finish her sentence; she began to cough heavily. Macid felt his heart, which was swinging back and forth between rage and pity, filling with bitterness. He looked out the window:

"Yes, you're right," he said, and waited for Nigâr to get up and leave.

Anyway, Nigâr didn't intend to stay much longer. From the moment that Macid had said "you're going to stay here!" an anxious gloom had descended on her heart, and this place had begun to appear confining and dangerous. She thought to herself, "God forbid. How can I stay here? Again the old faces, names, conversations. Old memories..." and the resolution that seemed to Macid to be a rescue, was for her a condemnation that already jolted her. However, it's not that the desire to see her children and live with them didn't occupy her heart at all. She asked Macid:

"When are they coming? Will they be with their father?"

The young man was biting his lip out of anger:

"You're completely out of it. Didn't I just tell you a moment ago?"

Nigâr bowed her head in a sad and innocent way.

"Forgive me, brother," she said. "I don't know why I'm so disoriented, my nerves are a wreck. I think I've got a fever."

As she said this, she stood up slowly. Macid directed her to the door without saying a word. When they were about to part ways, Nigâr said:

"Please don't forget to send me word a few days before they come! Maybe by then, I can convince Nur Baba."

The young man nodded his head without saying a word and only shook Nigâr's hand.

Bibliography

Ataman, Sadi Yaver. *Atatürk ve Türk Musıkisi*. Ankara: Kültür Bakanlığı, 1991.

Baydar, Mustafa. "Karaosmanoğlu, 'Nur Baba,' Rıza Nur ve 'Atatürk' üzerine açıklamalar yapıyor." Milliyet, December 20, 1974.

Birge, John Kingsley. The Bektashi Order of Dervishes. London: Luzac, 1937.

——. *The Bektashi Order and Bektachiyya: Études sur l'ordre mystique des bektachis et les groupes relevant de Hadji Bektach*, edited by Aleksandar Popović and Gilles Veinstein. Istanbul: Ed. Isis, 1995.

Canım, Rıdvan. *Türkiye Diyanet Vakfı İslam Ansiklopedisi*, "Sâkînâme." İstanbul: TDV İslam Araştırmaları Merkezi, 2009.

Çelebi, Evliya. *An Ottoman Traveller: Selections from the Book of Travels of Evliya Çelebi*. Translated and edited by Robert Dankoff and Sooyong Kim. London: Eland, 2011.

Clayer, Nathalie. "Sufi Printed Matter and Knowledge about the Bektashi Order in the Late Ottoman Period." In *Sufism, Literary Production, and Printing in the Nineteenth Century*, edited by Rachida Chih, Catherine Mayeur-Jaouen and Rüdiger Seesemann, 351–367. Würzburg: Ergon-Verlag, 2015.

Coakley, Sarah, ed. *Religion and The Body*, Cambridge Studies in Religious Traditions, Volume 8. Cambridge, UK: Cambridge University Press, 2000.

De Jong, Frederick and Bernd Radke. *Islamic Mysticism Contested: Thirteen Centuries of Controversies and Polemics*. Leiden: Brill, 1999.

Demir, Ahmet. "Yakup Kadri Karaosmanoğlu'nun Nur Baba'sı için Döneminde bir Reddiye: Nur Baba Masalı." *Türk Kültürü ve Hacı Bektaş Veli Araştırma Dergisi* 80 (2016): 51–77.

Dressler, Markus. *Writing Religion*. Oxford: Oxford University Press: 2013.

Ernst, Carl. *The Shambhala Guide to Sufism*. Boston, MA: Shambhala Publications, 1997.

Gariper, Cafer and Yasemin Küçükcoşkun. "II. Meşrutiyet Döneminde Yayımlanan Nur Baba Romanı ve Yarattığı Akisler." *Bilig/Türk Dünyası Sosyal Bilimler Dergisi* 47 (2008): 45–78.

Göknar, Erdağ. "The Novel in Turkish: Narrative Tradition to Nobel Prize." In *The Cambridge History of Turkey*, Volume 4, edited by Reşat Kasaba, 472–503. Cambridge, UK: Cambridge University Press, 2008.

Gür, Deniz Ali. "Ahmet Rıfkı (1884–1935): A Francophone Bektashi in the Late Ottoman Empire." Unpublished MA thesis, Central European University, 2021.

Hâşim, Ahmet. "Yakup Kadri Nur Baba Münasebetiyle," *Akşam*, no. 1305, 9 Mayıs 1338/May 9, 1922: 3.

Jäschke, Gotthard. "Die Frauenfrage in der Türkei." *Saeculum* 10. JG (1959): 360–369.

Kara, Cem. *Grenzen überschreitende Derwische: Kulturbeziehungen des Bektaschi-Ordens 1826–1925*. Göttingen: Vandenhoeck & Ruprecht, 2018.

Karamustafa, Ahmet T. "Kaygusuz Abdal: A Medieval Turkish Saint and the Formation of Vernacular Islam in Anatolia." In *Unity in Diversity* edited by Orkhan Mir-Kasimov, 329–342. Leiden & Boston, MA: Brill, 2014.

——. *God's Unruly Friends: Dervish Groups in the Islamic Later Middle Period, 1200–1550*. Oxford: Oneworld, 2006.

——. *Sufism: The Formative Period*. Edinburgh: Edinburgh University Press, 2007.

Karaosmanoğlu, Yakup Kadri. *Gençlik ve Edebiyat Hatıraları*. Ankara: Bilgi Yayınları, 1969.

——. *Flamme Und Falter: Ein Derwisch-Roman*. Translated by Annemarie Schimmel. Gummersbach: Florestan, 1947.

——. *Nur Babá*. Translated by Alín Salom. Barcelona: Destino, 2000.

——. *Nur Baba*. Translated by Fetah Sulejmanpašić. Sarajevo: 1957.

——. *Nur Baba*. Translated by Giampiero Bellingeri Fabula. Milano: Adelphi, 1995.

——. *Ο τεκές του Νουρ Μπαμπά ή Κατήχηση στον έρωτα: μυθιστόρημα*. Translated by Giorgos Salakidis. Thessalonikē: Stamoulēs Ant, 2009.

Karaosmanoğlu, Yakup Kadri. *Nur Baba*. İstanbul: Orhaniye Matbaası, 1923.

Kayaalp, Nilay. "Pera'nın yersiz yurtsuz kahramanları: Vallauri ailesi, Edouard Lebon, Alexandre Vallauri ve M. Vedad Tek," MA thesis, Yıldık Teknik Üniversitesi, 2008.

Kaygusuz, Bezmi Nusret. *Nur Baba Masalı*. İzmir: Ahenk Matbaası, 1338/1922.

Koçak Hemmat, Ayşe Özge. *The Turkish Novel and the Quest for Rationality*. Leiden: Brill Rodopi, 2019.

Koçu, Reşad Ekrem. "Baker (George)." In *İstanbul Ansiklopedisi*, Volume 4, 1886–1887. İstanbul: İstanbul Ansiklopedisi ve Neşriyat Kollektif Şirketi, 1960.

Köse, Yavuz. "Vertical Bazaars of Modernity: Western Department Stores and Their Staff in Istanbul (1889–1921)." *International Review of Social History* 54, no. 17 (2009): 91–114.

Maden, Fahri. "Çamlıca'da bir Erenler Durağı: Tahir Baba Tekkesi." In *Uluslararası Üsküdar Sempozyumu VII: 1352'den Bugüne Şehir*, edited by Süleyman Faruk Göncüoğlu, 220–250. İstanbul: 2012.

——. "Sütlüce'de bir Bektaşi ocağı: Caferabad (Bademli-Münir Baba) Tekkesi." *Alevilik Araştırmaları Dernegi* 5 (2013): 155–174.

Noyan, Bedri. *Bütün yönleriyle Bektâşîlik ve Alevîlik: Vol. VI Ünlü Bektaşiler ve Bektaşi fıkraları*. Ankara: Ardıç Yayınları, 2003.

Öztürk, Serdar. "Türk sinemasında ilk sansür tartışmaları ve yeni belgeler." *Galatasaray Üniversitesi İletişim Dergisi* 5 (2006): 47–76.

Popović, Aleksandar and Gilles Veinstein, eds. *The Bektashi Order and Bektachiyya: Études sur l'ordre mystique des bektachis et les groupes relevant de Hadji Bektach*. İstanbul: Édition Isis, 1995.

Procházka-Eisl, Gisela, "Andelib, Mehmet Esat," in Encyclopaedia of Islam, Volume 3. http://dx.doi.org/10.1163/1573-3912_ei3_COM_27322

Schick, İrvin Cemil. "Hz. Ali ve Devesi Levhaları" in *Deve Kitabı* edited by Erkan Demir and Emine Gürsoy Naskali, 5–40. İstanbul: Kitabevi Yayınları, 2014.

Schiffer, Reinhold. *Oriental Panorama: British Travellers in 19th Century Turkey*. Amsterdam: Rodopi, 1999.

Schimmel, Annemarie. *Mystical Dimensions of Islam*. Chapel Hill: University of North Carolina Press, 1975.

Siriyyeh, Elizabeth. *Sufis and Anti-Sufis: The Defense, Rethinking and Rejection of Sufism in the Modern World.* London: Routledge–Sufi Studies Series, 1998.

Soileau, Mark. "Spreading the Sofra: Sharing and Partaking in the Bektashi Ritual Meal." *History of Religion* 52, no. 1 (2012): 1–30.

Tanpınar, Ahmet Hamdi. *Edebiyat Dersleri.* İstanbul: Yapı Kredi Yayınları, 2002.

Üsdiken, Behzat. "Baker Mağazaları." in *Dünden Bugüne İstanbul Ansiklopedisi Volume* 1. İstanbul: Ana Basım, 1993.

——. "Bonmarşeler." in *Dünden Bugüne İstanbul Ansiklopedisi*, Volume 1. İstanbul: Ana Basım, 1993.

Wilson, M. Brett. "The Twilight of Ottoman Sufism: Antiquity, Immorality, and Nation in Yakup Kadri Karaosmanoğlu's *Nur Baba*," *International Journal of Middle East Studies* 49 (2017): 233–253.

Zarcone, Thierry. *Secret et sociétés secrètes en Islam: Turquie, Iran et Asie centrale, XIXe–XXe siècles: franc-maçonnerie, carboneria et confréries soufies.* Milan: Arché, 2002.

Index

For Product Safety Concerns and Information please contact our EU
representative GPSR@taylorandfrancis.com
Taylor & Francis Verlag GmbH, Kaufingerstraße 24, 80331 München, Germany

www.ingramcontent.com/pod-product-compliance
Lightning Source LLC
Chambersburg PA
CBHW071128100726
47908CB00008B/2534